> ## "I never gave up hope of finding real magic."

She risked a glance at Connor to see how he was taking her revelations. Would he be incredulous, condescending, amused?

No, he wore a look of tender understanding that made her heart turn over in her breast.

He took her face in his hands and stroked her cheek with his thumb. "I'll help you, lass," he promised. "I'll help you find your magic."

Mesmerized by the sincerity and intensity of his declaration, P.J. leaned toward him and tilted her face up in wonder. "You will?" she breathed.

"Yes, I will," he affirmed and bent to kiss the lips she so trustingly offered him.

Dear Reader,

You're about to meet one of the most mysterious, magical men!

Connor O'Flaherty is many things, but none of them is ordinary, as P. J. Sheridan—and you—are about to find out.

And neither are any of the heroes in American Romance's ongoing series MORE THAN MEN. Whether their extraordinary powers enable them to grant you three wishes or live forever, their greatest power is that of seduction.

So turn the page—and be seduced by Connor O'Flaherty.

It's an experience you'll never forget.

Regards,

Debra Matteucci
Senior Editor & Editorial Coordinator
Harlequin
300 E. 42nd St.
New York, NY 10017

Pam McCutcheon

A LITTLE SOMETHING EXTRA

Harlequin Books

TORONTO • NEW YORK • LONDON
AMSTERDAM • PARIS • SYDNEY • HAMBURG
STOCKHOLM • ATHENS • TOKYO • MILAN
MADRID • WARSAW • BUDAPEST • AUCKLAND

For Mom and Dad, who were so enthusiastic about my
screwy leprechaun story, with thanks to Pikes Peak
Romance Writers for inspiring the orange scene, to
Dick Gandolf for the pepper, and to the Wyrd Sisters
for laughing in all the right places.

ISBN 0-373-16614-1

A LITTLE SOMETHING EXTRA

Copyright © 1996 by Pam McCutcheon.

Chapter One

"Y'know," Amaranth said as she plucked the lone orange from the fruit bowl on the restaurant table and gazed at it thoughtfully, "sex is like an orange."

P. J. Sheridan groaned. This was why she'd been so reluctant to accept her sister's lunch invitation. Amaranth's penchant for making her mystical pronouncements in a clear and carrying voice could be embarrassing at times.

Of course, P.J. knew Amaranth didn't mean to embarrass her, she just lived in a different world, one where everything had a mystical connection to everything else. It was Amaranth's way of trying to make sense of the universe and her place in it, to find where she fit into the scheme of things. Most people thought P.J.'s sister was a flake. She wasn't, not really. She was an intelligent, caring person—she just had a touch too much gullibility, that's all.

Amaranth's time-lost hippie look didn't help. She would've been unremarkable in the midst of a sixties peace rally, but here, in the haute monde surroundings of the chic restaurant, she looked strange and out of place. P.J., on the other hand, casually yet classically attired, would have fit in anywhere. It helped in her profession.

Amaranth eyed the orange once more and opened her mouth to speak. P.J. glanced quickly around the restaurant. Damn. There were two elderly women sitting at the next table. With her luck, they'd have perfect hearing. Her only hope was to destroy Amaranth's inspiration.

Tearing the orange from her sister's loose grasp, P.J. dug her nails into the depression next to the stem and peeled away an irregular patch of rind.

Amaranth leaned forward and watched the operation with rapt interest. "You see, the unpeeled fruit is like a man's body, ripe for desire—and you are his lover, stripping away the protective trappings of civilization."

P.J. examined her would-be lover and giggled despite herself. This poor guy was pockmarked all over his body and had a smeared blue Sunkist stamped on his derriere.

She'd better change the subject. Fast. "Okay, Sis. You asked me to lunch. What did you want to talk about?"

"Hmm?" Amaranth just continued to gawk as P.J. finished peeling the orange and dropped the spent pieces of rind on the plate in front of her.

Earth calling Amaranth. Come in, Amaranth. "Sis?"

"Oh, yeah," Amaranth said vaguely. "A man came into the shop. Said he wants to hire you."

Amaranth and their parents ran The Cosmic Connection, a successful New Age shop there in Vail, Colorado. Their clientele ranged from the very rich to the very strange. Chances were, this guy was one of the latter.

"Hire me? Amaranth, I'm a free-lance investigative reporter, remember? People don't just walk into a store and say they want to hire you. It isn't done that way."

Amaranth shifted her otherworldly gaze from the orange to P.J.'s face. "It isn't? Maybe he needs help with, you know, bookkeeping."

P.J. sighed. She only maintained the shop's records because her sister and parents didn't seem to recognize the importance of such mundane chores. P.J. loved her family, but their habit of living in a fantasy world grated on her nerves sometimes. "I doubt he wanted to hire me to do his books, either," she explained patiently. "Did he *say* what he wanted me for?"

Normally P.J. wouldn't care, but she hadn't sold a story in weeks and her bills had become rather pressing. If there was a chance this guy was on the level . . . well, she needed the money.

Amaranth screwed up her face in thought. "Uh-uh," she said finally.

"Well, did he at least leave his name?"

Amaranth brightened. "Yes. Yes, he did."

"Okay, what is it?"

"Uh, I don't remember."

P.J. sighed again, resigning herself to the inevitable game of twenty questions before she'd learn who this guy was and what he really wanted.

"Wait," Amaranth said. "I just remembered—he gave me a card." She rummaged inside her macramé handbag and unearthed a dog-eared business card.

"Here," she said, handing the card to P.J. as proudly as if it were a Pulitzer prize.

P.J. suppressed the urge to pat her sister on the head and perused the card: *Connor O'Flaherty. Something Extra. Fantasy Shoes Designed for Your Unique Personality.* Oh, yes, the new store in town. She gave her sister an incredulous look. "A *shoe* salesman?"

Amaranth squinted at the card. "There's something written on the back."

P.J. flipped it over. The handwriting was bold and masculine: *Ms. Sheridan, I have a story and a proposition for you on your favorite subject: magic. If you're interested, please come by my office anytime to discuss it. I promise you won't regret it.*

He certainly knew how to get her attention. Magic—real magic—was what she'd searched for all her life, and never found. She'd developed a reputation as an unbiased reporter of psychic phenomena because her inquisitive nature wouldn't give up until she'd proved or debunked promising stories of magic or mysticism. Unfortunately she hadn't been able to authenticate any of them so far.

It was enough to make anyone a cynic—anyone but P.J. She'd give this guy the benefit of the doubt until she heard what he wanted. First thing Monday she'd look him up.

Absently, P.J. popped an orange section into her mouth. As she bit into it, the cool, sweet liquid gushed over her tongue. She squeezed all the juice out with her teeth and swallowed it, leaving the depleted pulp in her mouth.

Yuck. It tasted like wet, soggy string. How could people swallow this stuff? Surreptitiously she spit the pulp into a napkin and glimpsed Amaranth's enthralled expression as she stared at the remnants of the orange. *Uh-oh.*

"You *do* see it, don't you?" Amaranth asked. "As you join together in sweet ecstasy, you become one in a simple act as old as time itself."

Thank goodness this was a navel orange. No telling what analogies Amaranth would've drawn if there'd been seeds in it. To distract her sister from further contemplation of her navel, P.J. covered the spent rind with another napkin.

Too late. Amaranth gazed sadly at the litter on the table. "And when it's over—"

"Never mind." P.J. suppressed a giggle. After all, it hadn't been too bad—the old ladies had only sent one curious glance their way. Maybe she could escape without further embarrassment after all.

P.J. quickly wrapped up the debris and deposited it on the tray of a passing busboy. So much for lover boy.

She turned back to face her sister and recoiled in horror. Flourishing a banana in P.J.'s face, Amaranth said, "Y'know—"

P.J. fled.

TWO DAYS LATER, after P.J. apologized to Amaranth for deserting her and patiently endured another soliloquy on the role fruit played in the cosmic scheme of things, she decided to look up the shoe salesman.

Entering the Swiss-inspired building where Something Extra had their offices, she walked up the stairs to the second floor and glanced around, pleasantly surprised. It was different from what she'd expected.

Maybe she was wrong—maybe this O'Flaherty was one of the very rich instead of one of the very strange. It would certainly be a nice change.

She approached the receptionist and glanced at her nameplate. "Hello, Glenna, I'm P. J. Sheridan. I have an appointment with Mr. O'Flaherty."

"Oh, yes," the perky redhead said. "You're early. He's out for a moment, but he'll be right back. Please, won't you wait in here?"

Glenna ushered P.J. into an elegant office that commanded a wonderful view of the ski slopes, blissfully free of snow this time of year. Unfortunately they wouldn't be for long. Nature's lush green beauty would soon give way to dirty snow and the ugly tracks of rabid skiers. In silent protest P.J. had refused to learn to ski.

She turned her attention back to her plush surroundings, feeling a little out of place. Having expected the man to be one of the very strange, she'd worn her tight faded jeans and a white ruffled poet's shirt. With her long black hair feathered back from her face and hanging to her waist, she looked as though she belonged at The Cosmic Connection herself.

It was intentionally deceiving. Most people who knew her family ran a New Age shop took one look at her in this outfit and treated P.J. the way they treated her sister—as someone not quite all there. It was a useful camouflage in a profession where she met all sorts of self-proclaimed mystics. It made them feel more relaxed, more willing to open up around her. Besides, it was comfortable and she liked it.

But glancing around at the posh appointments of this office, she wished she'd worn something different. Something extra? The door opened, catching P.J. in midchuckle.

The chuckle died in her throat as she took in the giant standing there. He was gorgeous. Tall, with rumpled red-gold hair and broad shoulders filling out a tailored silk suit, he had the greenest eyes she'd ever seen. This was a shoe salesman? *Take my feet, please!*

He smiled back at her, revealing an engaging dimple. "Ah, so you'll be Miss Sheridan?"

What a lovely accent. His voice was as smooth and deep and rich as Irish whiskey—and just as intoxicating. She nodded and somehow maintained the presence of mind to hold out her hand. "Yes, I'm P. J. Sheridan. Mr. O'Flaherty?"

He took her hand and shook it gently yet firmly. "The same," he said with a twinkle in his beautiful eyes. "P.J.? Is that your full name or will it be standing for something else?"

"No, it stands for—" P.J. halted, shocked. She'd been so mesmerized by the sheer physical presence of this man that she'd almost revealed her real name. *Nobody* knew her real name, except her family, of course. "It stands for...something else. I'd rather not discuss it."

For one thing, it was embarrassing. For another, if the legends were true, entrusting someone with her true name would give that person power over her. Though she hadn't been able to prove magic was real—yet—P.J. hedged her bet and kept her name to herself.

He nodded, amiably accepting her answer. "Won't you have a seat, then?"

P.J. gratefully sank onto the nearby wing chair. The big Irishman leaned against the front of his desk and crossed his ankles, still smiling at her. Curious as to what kind of shoes the owner of a fantasy shoe store would wear, P.J. glanced down at his feet.

Penny loafers. How... ordinary. If he designed shoes to fit people's personalities, just what did penny loafers say about *him?*

He spoke, drawing her attention back up to his smiling face. "Now, you'll be wanting to know why I asked you here?"

P.J. nodded. She was curious, and she could listen to his lovely Irish accent all day long.

"I'm very familiar with your work, y'see. You're a fair woman, Miss Sheridan, when it comes to psychic investigations, neither believin' nor disbelievin' until you uncover the true facts of the case."

He seemed to expect some reaction from her, so P.J. nodded again. The twinkle in O'Flaherty's eyes brightened and he cocked his head to one side. "That's why I'd like you to help me," he said.

P.J.'s heart did a little extra pitter-patter. She'd love to help this man, get to know him better—a lot better. "Certainly, Mr. O'Flaherty."

His smile deepened. "Please, call me Connor."

The name fit him—strong and bold. "Certainly, Connor," she said, liking the sound of his name on her tongue. "And you can call me P.J."

"All right, P.J. Now, what I'm about to tell you may sound a wee bit... odd at first."

Odd? He was the picture of masculine normality.

He glanced at her anxiously and said, "You see, I'm fairy."

P.J.'s jaw almost dropped to the floor as she clutched the arms of the chair in disbelief. No, it couldn't be. Disappointment stabbed through her. She regarded him incredulously. "You mean you're..."

Connor burst out laughing. "No, no, lass. You misunderstand."

P.J. sighed in relief.

"I'm *faerie*." He spelled it for her. "One of the little people. A leprechaun, to be exact."

She burst out laughing. "I'm sorry, I thought you said leprechaun." She couldn't have heard him correctly, but what else could it be? What else could possibly sound like *leprechaun?*

He nodded, grinning. "Yes, I'm a leprechaun."

That did it. She had to get out of here. P.J. rose slowly to her feet. Shaking her head in denial, she backed toward the door. "No, no. Leprechauns are Irish—little people with pots of gold who make shoes...."

He spread his arms. "Well, I'm Irish and I make shoes."

She couldn't believe she was having this conversation. "So where's your pot of gold?"

He laid a finger against his nose. "Ah, now that would be tellin'."

He had to be putting her on. Okay, she'd play along. She grabbed his thick wrists in both hands. "All right, Mr. Leprechaun," she said smugly. "I've got you now. According to legend, you've got to tell me where you've hidden your pot of gold."

He chuckled. "Ah, lass, you've trapped me, you have. But I'm a modern leprechaun, you know. You sure you want to know where 'tis? It won't do you any good."

She nodded decisively. "Tell me where your gold is hidden."

He leaned down to whisper in her ear, his warm breath tickling the strands of hair on her neck. "I've got it hidden in...mutual funds."

She thrust him away. "Stop playing games with me."

The look on his face was serious. "I'm not playing games. I am a leprechaun."

"With your gold in mutual funds?"

"Well, yes. It makes it harder for those tricksy mortals to get at it, y'see."

"Yeah, right. But leprechauns are *little* people." She took in his full height—the man must be six feet four inches tall at least. "You're not exactly little, you know. What happened to you?"

He shrugged expressively. "I grew."

The twinkle in his eyes betrayed him, and P.J. glared at the overgrown faerie.

"No, lass, I'm sorry for teasin' you. The truth of the matter is, we leprechauns weren't all that small to begin with, y'see. And we've intermarried with mortals over the years until we're as tall as you are. Sometimes taller."

He had a pat answer for everything, but did he really expect her to believe he was a leprechaun?

He must've seen the skepticism on her face for he held up an admonishing finger. "You're supposed to be unbiased, remember? So, why don't you assume

I'm tellin' the truth for now, and save the investiga-tin' for later. All right?''

He was right—she wasn't being objective. But to hear such a bizarre statement come from such a nor-mal-looking man was disconcerting, to say the least. "Okay, but you'll have to show me proof." A sudden thought struck her. "Is that why you want to hire me?''

"Yes and no. Please, lass, sit yourself down. I promise I won't bite.''

P.J. felt herself flush as she resumed her seat in the wing chair. She'd like to see those even white teeth nipping their way down her... *No! Stop that,* she ad-monished her libido. She wasn't about to get involved with a man who thought he was a leprechaun, for heaven's sake.

Connor's lilt interrupted her musings. "I need to tell you a little more about our magic and how it works. The glamarye—''

"Glamarye? What's that?''

"'Tis the leprechaun magic. Most of us can cast only a sort of glamour, or glamarye, over an object or a person to make it appear something other than it is. 'Tis a seeming, you understand, not an actual change.''

"So you're basically illusionists? Like magicians?'' How disappointing. She'd hoped he was going to be more clever than that.

"Yes, but it seems real to the person it's happenin' to. They can't tell the difference between the gla-marye and reality.''

"You said most of you have only a little magic. What about the rest?''

"Well, our magic depends on our gold."

She raised an incredulous eyebrow. "Your mutual funds?"

"Right, lass. The more gold, or money, we have, the more magic we have. And the more magic we have, the stronger and more 'real' our glamarye."

"Okay," she challenged. "Prove it. Show me your magic."

"Ah, lass, I can't be doin' that."

"Why not? Afraid I'll prove you're a phony?"

Her challenge didn't seem to bother him one whit. "No, but the magic has a price. Y'see, each time I use it, some of my gold vanishes. If I use it too much, the power diminishes to the point where I don't have it when I really need it. And with inflation growing the way 'tis, I have to be very careful not to let it eat up all my magic."

She regarded him skeptically. "But surely a very small demonstration wouldn't hurt."

He shook his head. "I'm afraid not. Y'see, I promised my people I'd use the glamarye only when it was absolutely necessary. And since I've only had my position a month, I need to be right careful how I spend it. You don't get to be king of the little people by squanderin' their magical inheritance."

"You're their. . . king?"

He nodded and P.J. grimaced to herself. Great, now he had delusions of grandeur—royalty, no less. She'd better get out of there, fast. Rising once more, she turned toward the door. "I'm sorry, Mr. . . . Connor, but I don't think I can help you."

Connor strode to the door, blocking her exit with one long arm. "Now wait, lass. You haven't even heard me out."

She visually measured his height and breadth. There was no way she'd be able to shove her way past, so she might as well humor him. "Okay, let's hear it."

"I want to use your experience and reputation as a cover for an investigation of my own."

"And that is?"

"My sister's talisman has been stolen, and I need to be gettin' it back."

P.J. had a feeling she'd regret asking, but she did it anyway. "What kind of talisman, exactly?"

"Well now, each leprechaun has a bit of talisman gold he keeps about his person, y'see. 'Tis the focus for his magic and represents all the gold he's accumulated."

"Like what, for example?"

"It could be anything—a gold watch, a necklace, a bracelet, a key ring. Anything."

"Oh? What's yours?"

He held up his right hand. "My ring—the shield of the O'Flaherty clan."

"I see. And your sister's?" As he hesitated, P.J. pictured a delicate necklace, whimsical earrings or perhaps a stunning jeweled orb.

Connor looked sheepish. " 'Tis a shoehorn."

"A shoehorn? A *shoehorn?*" This situation was getting more ridiculous by the minute.

"Aye, 'tis necessary, y'see—to work her magic in the shop. The magic she adds to the shoes is the 'something extra' in our name."

"Magic shoes," she said flatly. He expected her to believe this?

"Yes, for some reason, we leprechauns do seem to have an affinity for footwear. My sister Stayle designs shoes to fit people's personalities. When she fits the shoes, she adds a little glamarye to enhance their best attributes and project their true qualities to those around them."

"So what if the person is basically rotten? Will the shoes project that?"

"Aye, but Stayle cannot abide letting her magic help someone like that, so she adds more glamarye to sort of push them in the direction of the right."

Ah, an inconsistency. "But doesn't that use up her magic?"

"Yes, but we cater to those with lots of gold to spare. We charge them twice what it costs her to make them, so each time she uses her magic, she's actually strengthening it."

P.J. gave up. He had an answer for everything— now it was interest-bearing magic, no less. "Okay, but you still haven't told me how you need my help."

"Ah, well, y'see, we've narrowed the suspects down to five people who were in the shop the day the talisman turned up missin'. They were the only ones who had access to the room we reserve for our special clients—those who order the 'something extra.'"

He leaned forward confidentially. "Now, lass, here's what I'd like you to do. Everyone knows we advertise that our shoes have magic, but nary a one really believes it. I'd like you to interview our five suspects for one of your stories to try and prove we're full of blarney."

This was certainly a new twist. "You want me to *prove* you're lying?"

He flashed that dimple again. "I want you to try, at any rate. Since none of the suspects have met me, I'll accompany you as your photographer. When I shake their hands and they come in contact with *my* talisman, I'll be able to tell if they've handled Stayle's."

"Why go through all that? Why don't you just use your magic to find it, if it's that important?"

"A talisman, by its very nature, is secretive and hard to find. 'Twould take a very great deal of magic indeed to locate one when we don't know for certain where 'tis. 'Tis far more cost-effective this way, y'see."

That didn't sound very promising. "And what is that cost, Mr. O'Flaherty? Just how much do you propose to pay me?"

"Connor," he corrected her, then named a figure that made her whistle.

"That's cost-effective? The magic must really be expensive."

"And since the suspects are located throughout the United States and Europe, I'll be payin' your expenses, too."

"Let me get this straight," she said. "You're going to give me a handsome salary and pay my expenses to travel all over the world, just to find a shoehorn?"

"Yes, a solid-gold *magic* shoehorn."

"And I can write the story any way I want, even expose you as a bunch of charlatans if that's how I figure it plays?"

"Yes, lass, even that."

P.J.'s natural caution asserted itself. "Your offer is very tempting, but I'd like a few days to think about it."

A frown creased the brow of the friendly giant. "Can you possibly see your way clear to makin' it one day, lass? We're in an awful bind without the talisman, y'see."

He certainly seemed sincere, and he wasn't really asking much. "All right, Mr. O'Flaherty," she said decisively. "I'll give you an answer tomorrow."

P.J. left the office, her reporter's mind already working. She had plenty of time to check him out, see if he had a police record, a history of mental illness, a wife....

Chapter Two

As the door closed behind P.J., Connor chuckled. It was easy to see that the skeptical and very lovely Miss Sheridan was wary. She had a right to be. Faerie folk—the Fae—didn't often reveal themselves to mortals, but in this case it was a calculated risk—a necessary one. He had to get Stayle's talisman back, and soon.

The object of his thoughts came bursting into the room, a miniature version of himself, with short, gamin-cut red-gold hair and a piquant face. "Connor O'Flaherty, what have you done?" Stayle shrieked at him.

Uh-oh. That was the problem with having one of the Fae as his receptionist. Glenna considered his doings as fair gossip for the rest of his people—especially his sister. Plastering an innocent look on his face, Connor said, "Why, nothin'. What is it you're blathering on about?"

Stayle planted her fists on her hips and glared at him. "You know what I'm talkin' about, Connor O'Flaherty, that reporter who was here. Are you really going to hire a mortal to find me talisman?"

"Now, now, lass, let me explain."

"You'd better explain, and quickly, too."

"Come now, Stayle, sit yourself down and relax." He led her to the couch in his office and shut the door.

She sat there stiffly, glaring at him with an uncompromising stare. "Well?"

"You know how expensive 'twould be to use magic to find the talisman—"

"And whose fault is that, I'd like to know? If you hadn't put that extra glamarye on it, 'twouldn't be so blasted expensive."

"Aye, but I didn't spend any more than I had to. My position is very precarious."

"I'll say! Your 'modern business ways' don't exactly endear ye to most of the faerie folk. They'll not be trusting ye much longer unless they see some results."

"I fully intend to keep my promises, but I can't if I squander my gold on finding your talisman."

"Squander, is it?" Stayle rose in outrage. "I'll have ye know—"

"Shut your gob," Connor said affectionately, "and hear me out. There's a better way of finding your talisman without spending so much gold and magic."

Stayle gave an unfeminine snort. "By hiring a mortal, I suppose."

"That's right. She's an investigative reporter and trained to be seekin' out information. What I'm payin' her is less than one-tenth of what it would cost to use my magic, and I can call in favors from the Fae to house and feed us in our travels."

"Why can't you hire one of our own kind?"

"Because none of us have the skill she does. Besides, my talisman led me to her as our best chance for success. And we don't know for sure she isn't our kind, y'know."

"And just what makes ye think she might be faerie?"

"Sheridan is a good Irish name, and she's the look of the black Irish about her. Long, dark hair, eyes as dark and bright as the starlit sky and a complexion as smooth as cream."

Stayle cocked her head speculatively. "Sounds like you're smitten, Connor me lad. Are you sure 'tisn't just your hormones talking?"

Aye, his hormones were talking loud and strong, but he never let them overpower his common sense or his responsibility to his people. "Nay, lass, I wanted to hire her *before* I met her."

Stayle's ire visibly faded as she glanced at Connor worriedly. "Still and all, she's probably mortal, y'know. And you promised you'd only marry a lass with faerie blood."

Yes, he had, and he meant it. He could hardly do anything less to meet his commitment to his people. "I know, I know. But just because I find her appealin' doesn't mean I plan to marry her."

Stayle raised an eyebrow. "I don't think—"

"I'm sorry, Stayle," he interrupted her gently. "But it's not your decision. As you reminded me, I'm the king of the Fae, and I say we find your talisman by hiring this mortal."

Her anger flared again. "You'd better be right, or I'll challenge your leadership meself."

Connor nodded. He wasn't really worried about Stayle's challenge, but if he didn't do this right, the rest of the Fae wouldn't be so understanding. The hereditary title of "king" was a misnomer; the Fae had borrowed the mortal system of democracy years ago, and he was subject to recall at any time. "I am right, you'll see," he reassured her. He had to be.

Stayle's expression turned pleading. "I...I need me talisman, Connor—soon. I can't keep the store open while I'm so worried—I can't concentrate. I'll try it your way, but only for a month. If you don't find it by then, promise me you'll use the magic, and to the devil with your position."

Connor clasped his sister's hands in his, feeling a bit guilty. Despite the torture she was going through, she still trusted him. He'd find that cursed talisman if it was the last thing he did. "Yes, Stayle, I promise. One month."

Stayle dashed a tear from her eye and strode out the door. Being Stayle, she couldn't resist having the last word. "And don't you go getting attached to that mortal, hear?"

Connor chuckled. With a little luck, P. J. Sheridan wouldn't prove to be totally mortal. Considering his instantaneous attraction to her, and her affinity for magic, she had to have some faerie blood. He'd bet on it.

P.J. PARKED HER CAR outside the pedestrian village and shrugged into her wool coat before making the short walk to Connor O'Flaherty's offices. She'd promised the man an answer today, and he'd get it . . . just as soon as she figured out what it was. She had a few questions she wanted to ask the oversize leprechaun first.

Leprechaun, indeed! P.J. had an open mind about the existence of magic, and preferred to give those she investigated the benefit of the doubt, but faeries?

Most of the stories she'd investigated had at least possessed some basis in logical physical laws or could be explained by the power of the subconscious mind—an observable scientific fact. But this man claimed his magic was based on the amount of cold, hard cash he had in the bank. It was just too ludicrous.

Be honest, she admonished herself as she walked down the steps toward Bridge Street. *It's not the type of magic that's bothering you—it's the man who's claiming it.* With his size and drop-dead looks, he didn't need to draw attention to himself. Why was he doing this?

P.J. could only come up with two possible explanations. Either he was suffering from a powerful delusion, or someone was playing an elaborate trick on her—someone who knew of her inquisitive nature and search for true magic.

But who? No one she knew had the wherewithal to pull off such a costly trick. And her investigation of O'Flaherty and his company showed they'd been in business for over six months—a long time to set up such a deception.

In a way, she hoped he was part of an elaborate scheme to deceive her. At least then she wouldn't have to worry about his mental health. No, to be honest, she didn't have to worry about that, either. Her investigation had shown no evidence of mental illness or a police record. She smiled secretly. There was no evidence of a wife or girlfriend, either.

P.J. sighed. Okay, so neither hypothesis seemed to fit. Whatever his reasons, Connor had offered her a lucrative job and she owed him an answer.

Yes, but in person? her conscience nagged at her. She could have asked her questions and given him her answer by phone just as easily. She didn't have to see him again.

But it was always easier to talk to someone in person, she argued back. Facial expressions and body language sometimes provided more information than mere words and inflection—something good reporters learned early on. So she really *needed* to see him, to get an idea of whether he was on the level.

But that didn't explain why she'd taken such care with her appearance this morning, why she'd worn her new gray flannel slacks with the expensive blouse. She just wanted to look...professional. Yeah, that was it. Professional.

Never mind that the icy pink blouse complemented her complexion nicely. Never mind that it made her hair look rich and shiny. Never mind that... Ah, hell. She wanted to look good for Connor O'Flaherty. She wanted him to think she was pretty. She wanted to knock him off his size-thirteen penny loafers.

There, she'd finally admitted it. Now she could go on with the interview without worrying about her own motives.

P.J. stopped in front of the clothing shop below Connor's office and considered what approach she should take. It would probably be best to act on the assumption he was a real leprechaun, or at least that *he* believed he was, and see where things went from there.

Having formulated her strategy, P.J. strode quickly up the stairs into the Something Extra offices and opened the door to find Connor O'Flaherty perched casually on the corner of his receptionist's desk. P.J. felt a momentary twinge of envy. They certainly looked cozy, she thought.

The two looked up as P.J. opened the door, and Connor straightened, giving her a genuine smile that lit his beautiful green eyes and made her feel as if she were the only person in the world. Her heart stopped beating for a moment, then resumed its pace four-fold. The man was just as devastating as she remembered. "P.J., it's so nice to see you again," he said warmly. "Have you come to give me your answer?"

"Yes, I have." P.J. kept her tone crisp and businesslike to keep from revealing just how attractive she found this man. "But I have a few more questions first."

"Well, then, shall we go into my office?"

He ushered her into his office, and P.J. tried to ignore the speculative look Glenna gave them before Connor shut the door. What did the woman's look mean? Was she jealous? Or, worse, had she divined P.J.'s growing infatuation with her handsome boss? Neither supposition was very palatable, and P.J. pushed them to the back of her mind.

She took off her coat and sat down, feeling rewarded by Connor's appreciative sidelong glance. "Now, what can I tell you, lass?"

P.J. cleared her throat nervously. "Your offer is very tempting, Mr. O'Flaherty—"

Disappointment flooded his countenance. "I thought you'd agreed to call me Connor."

She had, but "Connor" sounded so intimate, and she didn't quite trust herself to be that familiar—yet.

It was even more difficult to disappoint him.

"All right…Connor." He rewarded her with a wide, open smile that was difficult to resist. "Your offer is very tempting, but I'm confused about a few things, so I have some questions to ask you."

"Fire away, lass," he said in his wonderful Irish lilt.

"Well, first of all, why do you have an accent? According to my research, you were born and raised here in the United States and have been to Ireland only on short trips."

Not at all perturbed by the revelation that she'd been checking him out, Connor said, "Well, it's like this, lass. Y'see, my people came to Colorado in the 1859 gold rush. I'm sure you can understand why."

His twinkling green eyes invited her to share his amusement. "To get more gold to increase your magic, I suppose."

"Of course. Well, we did quite well seeing as how we have an affinity for the yellow stuff, and many of our brethren followed us across the ocean from Ireland to make their fortunes, too. Being so far from home, we sort of stayed close together, tight knit, you'd say. And, naturally, the love of Ireland brought us closer. No matter where they live, the Fae feel a kinship for the Emerald Isle, and we keep her traditions and language alive."

His lips curved into a dreamy smile and his eyes focused beyond the room, as if on the vision of a distant land only he could see. He murmured, "There's an old Irish blessing that says, 'There's music in the Irish names Kilkenny...Tipperary.... There's beauty in the countryside, from Cork to Londonderry. And whoever makes his home close to Irish sod has found a bit of heaven and walks hand in hand with God.'"

The warmth in his voice as he spoke the simple words of the blessing brought a lump to P.J.'s throat.

Connor shook off his momentary preoccupation and smiled down at her. "Besides, Gaelic is the language of glamarye, y'see. We speak it at home to keep in practice."

P.J. cleared her throat and nodded. "Okay, now if I'm going to help you find your sister's talisman—"

"If, is it?"

Her answering look was steady, measuring. "Yes, if. I haven't quite decided whether to take this on yet. It all depends on your answers to my questions." She had to convince herself there really was a viable story here, that she wasn't taking the assignment merely to be close to Connor O'Flaherty. That *would* be unprofessional.

"That sounds fair enough," he said. "What is it you're wantin' to know?"

From experience, she knew most charlatans were very good at rationalizing why their magic worked, but were usually fuzzy on the how of it. That's where they were most vulnerable. "If we're going to search for this...shoehorn, I need to know more about how talismans work, and, in particular, how Stayle's works."

"All right. You remember I said each leprechaun's magic depends on how much gold he has?" At her nod, he continued. "Now, you'll understand 'tis a wee bit awkward to be carrying around your pot o' gold all the time.''

The twinkle was back in his eyes, but P.J. didn't trust it. She couldn't tell if he was putting her on or if he was merely amused. "I imagine it would be," she agreed dryly.

"So, over the centuries, we've perfected the development of the talisman to symbolize our wealth. This token, properly enchanted, allows us to focus our power and channel the magic through it without having to be in close proximity to our gold.''

"So why can't your sister just use it wherever it is? Doesn't it still have the power to focus her magic?"

"No, unfortunately, we have to be in actual physical contact for the talisman to work at all. That's why most are worn as jewelry—to ensure 'tis close all the time.''

"Then why on earth did Stayle choose a shoehorn as her talisman?"

"She didn't. I did." He sighed heavily and his expression turned morose. "I guess you'd better understand this too, lass. The power of the faerie folk is fadin'. We've intermarried with mortals so much over the years that our magic has become diluted and scarce. Most of those who have faerie blood don't even know they have it.''

"So what does this have to do with the shoehorn?"

He grinned disarmingly. "I'm gettin' there, lass. When I was chosen as leader, I promised to do what I could to bring more magic back into our race, by finding a way to identify those with faerie blood. That's when I came up with the idea for the boutique and the shoehorn.''

His logic was becoming difficult to follow. She shook her head in confusion.

"Y'see, faerie folk, whether they realize what they are or not, are always attracted to magic. Usually the more magic they have, the more successful they are, and therefore the more likely to be able to afford our expensive shoes. We opened the boutique hoping our first customers would be the Fae. We didn't count on the fact that rich mortals are just as attracted by the idea and can also well afford our product."

"So how do you tell them apart?"

"Ah, there's the rub. You can't, really, unless you cast an enchantment on a talisman to tell you which is which. So, since Stayle is the one who comes into contact with the customers and fits the custom-made shoes, I convinced her to change her talisman to something innocuous, something she could touch customers with easily, but that I or others could use if necessary."

"Hence the shoehorn."

"Exactly. She uses the talisman to fit the shoes, and if the customers have faerie blood, they're surrounded by a sparkling gold aura that only other Fae can see."

P.J. had to admit it was all very logical and well thought out. At least if it was a delusion, it was a consistent one. "So why don't you just go around touching everyone with it and see how many auras you spark?"

Connor grimaced ruefully. "I wish 'twere that easily done. Y'see, I had to use up quite a bit of glamarye to set that enchantment, and every time Stayle uses it, some of my magic is used up, too. I'd rather use it only on those who are more likely to be faerie."

"And if they show up in your shop looking for magic shoes and can afford them, they're more likely to be faerie."

"Right."

"How many have you found?"

His face fell. "Only one so far, but I'm hopin' as word gets around we'll find more."

The light dawned. "Ah, I see. That's why you want me to write the article—to get the word out."

"That's right, and I'll not care if you scoff at our claims or no. When the Fae get a hint of the possible existence of faerie magic, they'll show up to find out for themselves."

"And that's why you don't object to a real investigation of your claims."

He nodded and smiled, flashing that dimple again. P.J.'s emotions surged in response, bringing her body to tingling awareness.

Good grief, that smile of his was lethal. Forcing her mind back to the discussion at hand, P.J. realized with a frisson of guilty pleasure that there wasn't anything to keep her from pursuing the story if the rest of his story held water. "How did you narrow down the suspects to just five people?"

"They were the first customers to order custom-made shoes, and Stayle scheduled them all for fittings on the same day. They were the only ones who entered the workroom where she fits the special shoes, so they were the only ones who could've seen the talisman. She used it during each fitting, and it didn't turn up missin' until after they all left. She left the workroom to answer the telephone, and when she came back, the shoehorn was gone."

"So how do you know someone didn't just walk in off the street and take it?"

He shrugged. "I don't, really. But you can't see the workroom from the street, so how could anyone else have known it was there? 'Twould appear it must be one of the five. Besides, 'tis the only lead we have."

His worried look seemed so genuine that P.J. had to concede he was either a very good actor or he really believed what he was saying. Her instincts told her he really believed it. "Okay, say one of these five does have it. Would he know what he has?"

Connor's brow furrowed in thought. "I don't think he'll know what 'tis he's stolen—or she—two of the suspects are women, y'know. Except... we identified one of them as having faerie blood. No, 'tis unlikely she'd know what she had. You can't really tell by look or feel that the talisman is magic—it appears to be just plain gold." He twisted the ring on his right hand. "Would you like to touch mine and see for yourself?"

P.J. shuddered. "No, thanks. I'm allergic to gold. For some reason, the mere touch of it on my skin gives me the creepy crawlies."

"Ah, you'll not be faerie, then."

P.J. was hard put to understand the disappointment in his voice. Raising an eyebrow, she said, "I think not. If what you say is true, it would be hard to imagine a faerie who's allergic to gold. So, you don't think the thief knew of the talisman's abilities?"

"No, I'd say the thief probably stole it for its monetary value. 'Tis solid gold, y'know."

Yes, and a sillier thing she couldn't imagine. She could see the advertisement now: Twenty-four-carat-gold shoehorn—the gift for the man who has everything. P.J. shook her head at the absurdity. "Okay, so what if the thief finds out what he has? Could he use it then?"

"Without Stayle's permission, he could use it only if he knew what he had, *and* knew where she hid her gold, *and* could rekey the talisman to himself."

"So it's highly unlikely?"

"Aye, lass, very unlikely."

"So why bother searching for it? Why not just make another and let him keep the silly thing instead of chasing all over the world after it?"

"Because it's keyed to Stayle, y'see. She can't access her magic without it, and that's mighty hard on a leprechaun, y'know. She can't make another without the loss of a great deal of gold—both mine and hers since the spell linked them together. I've promised to find it within a month, or use my own magic to locate it."

He gave her a direct look and one of those dimpled half grins of his. "So, lass, have you decided if I'm a fruitcake yet, or no?"

P.J. almost choked. "Yes...no. I mean, no, I haven't quite decided yet." At least if he was a fruitcake, he was a mighty consistent one. She squared her shoulders and gave him her best professional look. "I *am* trying to maintain my objectivity, Mr....er... Connor."

"How about my offer? Have you decided what you'll be doing about that?"

Common sense said the man was trouble. But common sense warred with her need to pay the bills—and it *was* a viable story. She hadn't gotten an offer like this in a long time. She couldn't pass it up.

And she couldn't pass up an opportunity to get to know Connor O'Flaherty just a little bit better, either. "Yes, I've decided to take you up on your offer, but I need a couple of days to come up with a plan, set up the interviews, that sort of thing. Is that okay with you?"

He beamed at her. "Aye, lass, so long as it doesn't take too long." He handed her a slip of paper. "Here are the names and addresses of the five suspects."

She took the list and tucked it into her pocket. "All right, Connor, you've got a deal. I'll call you in a couple of days."

She shook his hand to seal the agreement, feeling strangely as if she'd just taken the first step on an irrevocable life-altering journey. *Get a grip, Sheridan,* she chided herself. It's just another story, after all.

Chapter Three

Connor strode resolutely toward The Cosmic Connection, hoping to find P.J. inside. He wanted to learn more about the intriguing woman his talisman had led him to. She was such a mass of appealing contradictions—skeptical yet unbiased, shy yet bold, brusque yet soft and feminine. Which was the real woman? Maybe if he saw her in her own milieu, he could unravel the mystery that was P. J. Sheridan.

He pushed open the door of The Cosmic Connection and went inside. Delicate chimes announced his presence, and an older woman looked up from the counter with a smile. "I'll be right with you," she said as she rang up a customer's purchases.

Connor nodded and looked about the neat, orderly boutique with interest. He hadn't paid much attention to his surroundings the last time he was there. Now, though, he surveyed it all with interest, hoping it would provide him a clue to P.J.'s character.

It smelled like all New Age shops he'd ever been in—a strange blend of musk, patchouli and heavy, sweet incense. One small area to the right held dried herbs and flowers, but the rest of the shop seemed primarily devoted to books. Scattered here and there were crystals, runes, cards, amulets and other paraphernalia designed to help mortals simulate faerie magic.

He felt a slight tingling in his talisman ring. By chance, there was some powerful earth magic here, though how anyone could find the real thing amid all this misguided though well-meaning merchandise was anyone's guess.

The clerk handed the other customer her change, then walked over to Connor. "May I help you find something?"

Now that she was closer, Connor could discern the resemblance between this woman and P.J.—this must be her mother. "Yes, I've come to see P.J. Is she here?"

She looked about vaguely. "Yes, I believe she's in the office." She went to the stairs at the back of the shop and called up. "Pet? There's someone here to see you."

P.J. stuck her head out the door and peered down the steep steps. "Good grief, Mother. Why didn't you use the buzzer I—" She broke off when she spotted Connor, and a distinct look of annoyance crossed her face. "Oh, it's you. Well, don't just stand there. Come on up."

P.J.'s mother took in his full height and gave him a hesitant look, as if uncertain whether to let him near her daughter.

"Don't you be worryin', Mrs. Sheridan," he reassured her. "I'm not as heavy as I look. I'll lay odds the stairs will hold my weight."

She laughed, accepting his fabrication as her reason for hesitation. "Please, go on up, then. You'll find Pet in the first room on the right."

Pet? Was that her real name? Connor made his way up the narrow stairs, ducking to keep his head from hitting the ceiling, and turned into the office Mrs. Sheridan had indicated.

P.J. was there, hurriedly shoving some scattered papers from the top of the desk into a drawer. He didn't know why she bothered. The office was as untidy as the shop was neat. Papers and books spilled over every available surface, from the gray metal military-surplus desk and filing cabinets to the wooden chairs and bookcases. The state-of-the-art computer system was a jarring note in an otherwise old-fashioned and somewhat seedy-looking office.

P.J. glanced up with a look of apology. "Sorry, I always mean to clean the place up, but I never seem to have the time. . . ." She hesitated to give him an accusing look. "I told you I'd call you in a couple of days. It's been less than twenty-four hours. Why are you here?"

"Sorry, but I hadn't really planned to drop in. I was just in the area—" *Faith, how lame that sounded!* "I mean, I just thought I'd see how far you've come on settin' up the interviews and such. Pet, is it?"

She gave him an unmistakable glare. "No, it's not. My mother calls me that because she refuses to call me P.J. Says it makes me sound like a pair of pajamas."

Connor chuckled. "She's right. So if the *P* doesn't stand for Pet, what does it stand for? Petra? Patricia? Pamela?"

Her lips thinned. "I told you I didn't care to discuss it. Now, why don't we get down to business?"

Connor dropped the subject; it was obviously a sensitive one. "All right, how are you coming on setting up the interviews with our suspects?"

"I have calls in to all five of them," she explained briskly. "And they've all agreed to the interviews, but we haven't set up the exact times yet. I wanted to go over the strategy with you first. Here, sit down."

She cleared off one of the chairs by sweeping the pile onto the floor, and he perched uneasily on the ancient wooden structure. It looked so fragile, he wasn't sure it would bear his weight. "All right, what is your strategy, then?"

"Well, from what you've told me, the actress, Melissa Matthews, was the last one in the shop that day. I figure we'll start with her, since she's the one who saw the shoehorn last. She's still staying at her condo here in Vail, so she's also the closest."

Connor nodded. "Sounds reasonable. Then what?"

"If she's not the thief, we'll continue on to New York to see the stockbroker, then to Europe to visit the other three...." She trailed off, a pensive look on her face.

"What is it?"

She waved her hand vaguely. "Nothing, really, it's just odd that one of the suspects is Madame Cherelle. I've never met her, but we're in the same business—debunking, not reporting." She shot Connor a speculative look. "She hasn't already disproved your claims?"

"Nay, lass, how could she? She's the one who turned out to be faerie."

"Madame Cherelle—the famous psychic debunker—a faerie?" Disbelief echoed in P.J.'s voice. "How did she take the news?"

Connor shrugged. "I don't know, Stayle talked to her, I didn't."

"Well, it's all very strange, but what hasn't been since I met you?" P.J. laughed, then changed the subject. "So, what do you think of my itinerary?"

"It's fine, lass. Why don't you go ahead and finalize the interviews? Don't worry about hotels and plane reservations. I have...connections, family who'll be glad to help us out. Just let me know when and where we need to be and I'll make the arrangements."

P.J. nodded briskly and stood. Connor received the definite impression she was trying to rush him out of the store. He cocked his head, considering. Was she embarrassed about the shabbiness of the office or perhaps by the nature of what her family sold below stairs? Whatever it was, it was obviously making her uneasy.

That was the last thing he wanted to do. He remained seated, ignoring her hint. "Why don't you set things up and we'll discuss it over dinner tomorrow night?"

Pleasure warred with suspicion on her face. "Dinner? I don't think—"

"Now, lass, what harm could it do to have dinner with me?"

Her wary look didn't abate, but he had no intention of letting her professional scruples get in his way. "If we're going to be spending so much time together, we'll need to get to know each other—discuss how we're going to operate."

"Why don't we just discuss it in your office?"

"Because, although I'm fairly certain the thief is one of the customers, there's always the possibility it could be one of my staff, and I don't want to discuss our investigation in front of them."

She nodded slowly. She was buying it. Now for the clincher. He raised an eyebrow. "Of course, we could do it all here, if you'd rather...."

"No, no, not here," P.J. said hurriedly. "I guess dinner would be okay. Um, when...where?"

"I'll pick you up at seven." He managed to pry her address in West Vail out of her. "I'll see you then." He strode out of the shop, whistling.

It appeared his suspicions were correct. She didn't want him in her office—didn't want him to get to know the real P. J. Sheridan. That was too bad, because he intended to do so whether she liked it or not.

P.J. CHECKED HER WATCH for the eighth time. It was still only ten minutes to seven. She was habitually early for everything: appointments, meetings, dates. Unfortunately most people she knew were exactly the opposite. Connor probably was, too.

She checked her appearance in the hall mirror again. She'd taken special pains to give the right impression. Her simple black dinner suit with the black lace camisole top made her look professional but attractive. And her hairstyle added just the right touch. She'd piled it on top of her head in an elegant twist, allowing a few wisps of hair to escape to soften the effect.

P.J. nodded in satisfaction. She wasn't sure where he was going to take her to dinner, but chances were, it wasn't a hamburger joint.

Oh, Lord, she hoped he meant to serve her real food. She didn't know how she'd react if her new employer pretended to conjure up a faerie feast or something. She gave her reflection a dubious glance. Why was she going to so much trouble for a man who was so obviously off his rocker? Was it too late to call him and cancel the whole thing?

She reached for the phone but paused when she heard a car pull up outside. She checked her watch again. Five minutes to seven. She peeked out the window to see Connor emerge from the gray BMW parked outside her tiny apartment.

Ordinarily she'd be gratified to find a man who was as punctual as she was. But now... She dithered. Should she go with him or just pretend she wasn't at home?

Connor strode up the walk, looking perfectly normal in a conservative dark suit—and sexy as hell, too. P.J. quickly made up her mind. She pulled on her wrap and grabbed her briefcase, going out to meet him before he rang the doorbell.

She wasn't exactly ashamed of her little place, but any discretionary money she had didn't go into the house—it went into her wardrobe. She believed strongly in the dress-for-success principle and the importance of first impressions. So far it had worked very well for her, and she didn't want to spoil it by letting her new employer see her shabby, tiny apartment.

Besides, he'd already seen more than enough of her personal life when he'd invaded her office that morning. She didn't know or trust him well enough to let him any closer.

She met him on the sidewalk and said brightly, "I'm ready. Where are we going?"

He seemed a bit surprised at meeting her outside, but smiled and helped her into the car. "I hope you don't mind, but I've already made reservations."

He named one of the fanciest restaurants in town and she relaxed. "No, I don't mind. That sounds very nice." Though her family's shop was only a couple of blocks from the restaurant, she'd never eaten there. The establishments on that section of Gore Creek Drive were too expensive for her tight budget.

P.J. settled into the luxurious comfort of Connor's car, and he drove them across town, chatting lightly about ordinary things, putting her even more at ease. He pulled into the Vail Village parking garage and escorted her down to the pedestrian area. As they strolled companionably toward the restaurant, P.J. resolved to enjoy the evening. Connor was very attentive and it was almost possible to pretend they were on a real date—a far too infrequent occurrence of late.

As they neared the restaurant, she spotted a sign on the other side of the street. Right between a fur store and a shop selling crystal, Something Extra was spelled out in ornate letters above a display window.

"Wait," she said. "I want to see your merchandise." Though the shop was closed, the display was well lit. Inside were several pairs of fanciful shoes.

One pair caught her eye, and P.J.'s lips curved into a smile as she leaned closer for a better look. The flat-heeled shoes were made of delicate white netting, giving them a light, airy look. Dainty lace scallops arched around the foot, barely covering the toes, and a whimsical pink butterfly perched asymmetrically on the toe.

P.J. chuckled. The shoes appealed to her sense of whimsy. They didn't look as though they'd last an hour, and she'd never have the money to buy them—or the moxie to actually exhibit them in public—but wouldn't they be fun to wear!

"They're more sturdy than they look, y'know," Connor said with a smile.

"So, you're a mind reader, too, huh?"

He grinned. "Nay, 'tis what all the women say. But Stayle is a master at creating the illusion of ethereal, insubstantial shoes that are actually sensible and comfortable."

P.J. nodded and turned away from the display window. Connor escorted her across the street and into the posh restaurant, where P.J. was unsurprised to learn he was well-known. After they seated themselves and ordered, P.J. pulled out her briefcase.

Connor seemed surprised. "What's that, lass?"

"My notes on the itinerary. That's why we're here, isn't it?"

He flashed his dimple again. "Aye, but why don't we enjoy our dinner first and talk business afterward? That way we won't be spoiling our appetite."

P.J. shoved her files back in her briefcase. "Okay, you're the boss."

He took a sip of wine, his large strong hand somehow not looking at all incongruous on the delicate stem of the wineglass. "So, you know quite a bit about me, but I know very little about you, except that your family owns a New Age shop, you have a reputation for fairness and you're as lovely as the Emerald Isle on a frosty morn." His gaze turned serious, searching, though a half smile played around his mouth.

Good Lord, her fondest dream had come true—the man was flirting with her. P.J.'s insides quivered in disbelief and longing, and she took a sip of her wine just to have something to do with her hands and her mouth.

Her gaze turned back to his and he gave her a lazy smile. "So, lass, tell me why you agreed to my offer."

"Why?" She was proud of herself—her voice hadn't cracked a bit on the single syllable.

"Yes, why? You've obviously decided I'm not quite all there, and you have enough professionalism not to take my offer just for the money. So, why *did* you take it?"

P.J. felt her face flush in the wake of his searching gaze. Now what? She could hardly admit that the main reason she took it was because she wanted to see more—much more—of this drop-dead-gorgeous hunk.

Just then the waiter served her salad and offered her the pepper mill. She nodded, grateful for the interruption.

"Tell me when you've had enough," the waiter murmured.

He ground the pepper over her salad, and she'd just opened her mouth to tell him she'd had enough when the bottom fell out of the pepper mill. It landed in her salad with a thunk, and a stream of peppercorns rushed out to mound on her plate, then rolled off to bounce over every available surface of the table.

As the waiter and Connor looked on in horror, P.J. picked up her fork and said politely, "That's enough, thank you."

Connor burst out laughing, and the waiter breathed a sigh of relief, then bustled about, cleaning up the mess and apologizing profusely. He moved them to a different table, one nearer the window with a nice view of the softly lit street.

As the waiter deftly slid fresh salads in front of them, P.J. murmured, "I think I'll forgo the pepper this time, hmm?"

Crimson-faced, the waiter nodded and backed off. Connor chuckled. "It's a fair treat to see you have a sense of humor, lass. We'll get along just fine." His green eyes twinkled as he took a sip of his wine. "But you still haven't told me why you agreed to my offer."

The short interchange had given her a chance to formulate her answer. "I'm still building my reputation as an investigative reporter," she reminded him. "And this'll be a good way to do that. It's a terrific story with lots of different angles."

He smiled at her, curiosity and genuine interest plainly written upon his face. "Angles? I'm afraid I don't understand what you mean."

"Each time I write a story, I try to find as many markets as I can to sell it to. Regardless of the outcome of my investigation, I can usually write a dozen different stories, each with a slightly different slant, to sell to entirely different markets and readership."

"Like what, for instance?" he asked, obviously intrigued.

"Well, with a focus on your product, it might sell to a shoe-trade quarterly or a fashion magazine. Focus on the magic, and it might sell to a New Age magazine. Talk about the type of people who buy your product, especially if they're rich and famous, and celebrity magazines might buy it." She shrugged. "I'm sure there are lots more. I'll know better once the investigation is complete."

"So you don't write just psychic investigative pieces?"

She grimaced. "No, there isn't much market for such a narrow specialty—I couldn't afford to do that. I focus on magic when I can because it's what I enjoy."

He continued to ask questions to draw her out, and she chatted comfortably about her work and her family. Though they spoke of inconsequential things, Connor's warm friendliness and genuine interest encouraged her to open up. Over a delicious meal followed by a decadent dessert, they learned they both loved chocolate and caramel but hated nuts and coffee. Small things to build on, but it was nice to know they had something in common.

Finally getting around to the reason for the outing, Connor asked about her itinerary and they made arrangements to visit each suspect in turn. Then, having finished dinner and their business, Connor paid the bill and they reluctantly left the restaurant.

The wintry air outside was nippy, and P.J. pulled her wrap more tightly around her as they walked in companionable silence past the Children's Fountain, which was turned off for the winter, and down to the little covered bridge.

As she crossed it, P.J. slipped slightly on a patch of ice and Connor caught her arm to steady her, bringing her up close against his solid body. P.J. lingered for a moment in his welcome warmth, then reluctantly pulled away to lean on the wooden railing, her head slightly muzzy from his intoxicating nearness.

Her head cleared and she breathed deeply of the fresh air, drinking in the quiet charm of the gurgling stream flowing beneath the little wooden bridge, and the beauty of the mountain scenery cradling the small town. This was one of her favorite places in Vail.

Connor stood beside her and turned the conversation back to her work. "Why magic?" he asked softly. "Why did you choose to focus on it?"

"You've met my family. You must realize I've been surrounded by tales of magic all my life."

"Aye, but your family believes. You don't."

"No, but I *want* to believe. I love the idea of magic, I've just been . . . disillusioned—more than once."

She allowed a wistful smile to cross her face. This man was so easy to talk to, and the night itself was almost magical. A light dusting of snowflakes drifted down from the sky, painting the moonlit night with glittering stardust. Nearby, lovers strolled hand in hand, yet none came near enough to disturb their magic circle of contentment. It was almost as if they were isolated in their own small pocket of enchantment.

He covered her hand with his, warmth radiating from his strong palm and long fingers. "Would you care to tell me about it?"

She shrugged. "My first disillusionment came at the age of seven when Tommy Johnson told me Santa Claus and the Easter Bunny weren't real." She gave him a sad half smile.

He returned her smile gently, not amused or condescending, just waiting for the rest of the story.

"I didn't believe him at first, so I stayed up one Christmas Eve to prove him wrong. It was my first investigation and my first disappointment. Of course Santa Claus never showed up, it was just my parents pretending to be him, lying to me." She shrugged. "I don't know... the whole idea of magic was just so wonderful, exciting. In childhood you're ready and willing to believe in magic—in mystical beings like Santa Claus, the Easter Bunny and the Tooth Fairy." She glanced askance at him and raised an eyebrow. "One of your relatives, perhaps?"

He chuckled. "Nay, lass, I'm afraid the Tooth Fairy is pure myth."

P.J. sighed dramatically and laid a hand over her heart. "Another belief shattered." She stopped play-acting and turned serious. Somehow, discussing this with a man who believed he was a leprechaun didn't seem absurd at all. It seemed right and fitting. Who could better understand her quest for magic?

She gazed out at the chuckling stream and avoided his gaze. "But to a seven-year-old girl who longed to fly with Peter Pan and Tinkerbell, or to be rescued from a dragon by a handsome prince, it was quite a letdown to find out they weren't real. In fact, it was devastating." Even now the incident had the power to fill her with a sense of painful loss.

She risked a glance at Connor to see how he was taking her revelations. Would he be incredulous, condescending, amused?

No, he wore a look of tender understanding that made her heart turn over in her breast. Tipping her chin up with one finger, he asked gently, "And did you get over it?"

P.J. licked her dry lips. This man was beginning to weave his own kind of spell about her. "Oh, I survived, but I never gave up hope of finding real magic. I know it's out there somewhere—I just have to find it." She gave a self-deprecating shrug. "So, that's what I've been doing all my life."

Connor's face was mysterious and beguiling in the silvery evening shadows. He stroked her cheek with his thumb. "I'll help you, lass," he promised. "I'll help you find your magic."

Mesmerized by the sincerity and intensity of his declaration, P.J. leaned toward him and tilted her face up in wonder. "You will?" she breathed.

"Yes, I will," he affirmed, and bent to kiss the lips she so trustingly offered him.

The kiss was exquisitely tender—just the soft brush of his lips against hers and his remarkably gentle fingers caressing her cheek. No other part of their bodies touched. When she moaned and reached up to tangle her fingers in his thick hair, he tightened his arms around her and deepened the kiss, sending thrills chasing along her nerve endings.

Her body cheered, but her mind screamed no. No, this wasn't right. This man was her employer—and a deranged one at that. Reluctantly she pulled away and whispered, "We shouldn't be doing this."

Bringing her hand to his mouth, Connor brushed her knuckles with his lips, his eyes dark under the shadowed moon. "Aye, lass, mayhap you're right." He gazed deep into her eyes, then gently dropped another kiss on her upturned lips and took a step back.

P.J. admired his restraint. She doubted she'd have been able to break their embrace so easily, and she silently thanked him for doing what she lacked the strength to do.

He held out a hand. "We'd best be gettin' home."

She smiled and took his hand, feeling a little thrill course through her when he unselfconsciously threaded his fingers through hers and tugged her across the bridge toward the parking lot. All too soon they arrived at his car and he released her hand, helping her into the vehicle.

They chatted of the upcoming trip on the way home, acting as if nothing out of the ordinary had occurred—as if they hadn't just created their own special sorcery back on that bridge. It was a warm, comfortable feeling that P.J. was loath to see end. But end it did, and by the time they'd reached her home, they'd made arrangements to meet two days later to interview their first suspect.

As she climbed out of the car, Connor caught her hand again and favored her with a slow, lazy smile. In his wonderful lilting voice, he said, "I've another Irish blessing for you, lass. 'May good luck be with you wherever you go, and your blessings outnumber the shamrocks that grow.' Bless you, P.J., and I'll be seeing you later.''

P.J. stood in the cool evening air and watched as Connor drove away. What a wonderful man. She hugged the special enchantment of this night to herself. It was almost enough to make her believe in magic.

Almost.

Chapter Four

P.J. stood in front of her closet, indecisive. What should she wear today? She needed something that would present the image of a professional reporter, something that would make her look approachable enough so the suspect would open up and talk to her, yet not so severe that it would make her look unattractive.

She grimaced. Attractive. There was that word again. Until she'd met Connor O'Flaherty, she'd never worried about how desirable she looked.

Oh, he'd noticed her all right. P.J. blushed at the memory of their embrace. She'd been so caught up in his spell that she'd thrown caution to the faerie winds and practically begged him to kiss her.

He'd obliged her so sweetly, but the memory was pure torture. She played the events of that night over and over again in her mind. She couldn't decide: had he been merely polite, humoring her, or had he enjoyed it as much as she had? The uncertainty was agonizing.

And he was so damned amiable all the time, it was difficult to discern his real feelings. Too amiable, as far as P.J. was concerned. She'd bet she could call him nasty, filthy names and he'd just smile and nod and allow how she was probably right.

P.J. shook her head and turned her attention back to her closet. Blue. Blue inspired confidence. She pulled out her navy blue blazer and slacks and selected an open-necked blouse to go with them. The blouse added the right touch of casual appeal and just happened to be a flattering shade of aqua.

P.J. fussed over her appearance until she was satisfied, then had to hurry out the door so she wouldn't be late picking up Connor. She drove quickly to their arranged rendezvous in front of the Vail Village visitor's center and spotted him immediately.

He was hard to miss. He'd followed her instructions to dress down and was wearing a pair of well-worn jeans and a T-shirt, with a sports jacket casually draped from one hooked finger. With the camera bag slung around his neck, he was the image of the aspiring photographer.

She hadn't believed it possible, but he looked even more devastating now than he had in a suit. The T-shirt stretched tautly across his broad shoulders, hugging his muscular arms and chest and revealing a man who obviously kept in shape. His jeans snugged his slim waist and powerful thighs, faithfully outlining every inch of his impressive anatomy.

"Well, lass, do I pass muster?" Connor inquired as he leaned down next to her car window and flashed his dimple.

P.J. blushed again, hoping he hadn't noticed the direction of her gaze. "You'll do," she replied curtly, and unlocked the door so he could climb inside.

He squeezed his large frame into the small car, and P.J. immediately felt claustrophobic. Connor filled the compact import with the full force of his vitality, making her head swim with his intoxicating nearness. To keep her heartbeat on an even keel, she avoided looking at him and tried to ignore the effect his proximity was having on her.

Connor let out an exclamation of disgust. "Would you mind helpin' me here, lass?"

She turned to look at him and couldn't help but giggle. Her tiny car wasn't built to hold a man of Connor's heroic proportions. He was scrunched over in what had to be a painful position, his head denting the fabric of the car's roof. His legs were so long they were pressed up against the dashboard, and his chin was almost resting on his knees. He reminded her strongly of the genie in the movie *Aladdin*, stuffed into the "itty bitty living space" of his tiny lamp—only Connor's skin wasn't blue. Huddled in that position, he groped around on the right side of the seat.

P.J. unfastened her seat belt and leaned over him. "No," she said, "it's here." She reached over his knee to find the catch in front of his seat, and her senses were instantly engulfed by the power of his presence. Time slowed to a crawl as she registered the sensuous feel of his denim-clad legs against her breasts and inhaled his heady masculine scent. She froze for a brief, sweet moment, wishing she were back in his arms again.

"P.J.?"

She blushed. Lord, what did he think she was doing? P.J. shook herself out of her daze and back to the task at hand—the lever. Turning her head sideways to give her arm more room to maneuver under the seat, her eyes widened as she found herself nose-to-nose with Connor. Their breath mingled. With only a small movement, their lips would touch. Her hand tightened on the seat lever as she stilled, hoping he'd cross that tiny distance, yet dreading it, too.

"Ah, lass," he breathed, and turned his head to grant her wish.

Embarrassed, P.J. jerked back, and the seat shot back to its farthest length. Connor expelled a sign of relief and his eyes twinkled at her. "Was it as good for you as it was for me?"

P.J. could feel herself turn red, but she stopped from blurting out an apology just in time. What could she say? I'm sorry, but I really wasn't begging for another kiss? Pretending the incident hadn't happened, she said, "There's a lever on the right side that will bring the back down so you can straighten your neck."

He fumbled around on the right side of the seat and said, "I can't seem to find it. Would you mind helpin' me, lass?"

P.J. blushed at the thought of leaning her torso across his lap again. She gave him a wary look. It was just as she'd thought—the twinkle in his eyes gleamed unabated. He was teasing her again—in more ways than one. "Keep looking," she said tersely, and fastened her seat belt.

Connor found the lever remarkably quickly and reclined the seat. It still wasn't a perfect fit, but at least he looked a little more comfortable.

"Better?" she asked.

"Aye, at least now I don't think I'll be gettin' a cramp, anyway. Are you sure we can't take my car?" he asked in a plaintive voice.

"No, I represented myself as a free-lance reporter eager to make a few bucks. Your BMW would spoil the story. Besides, if we don't get going now, we'll be late."

He sighed in resignation and fastened his seat belt. "All right, let's go. But I beg you, don't be takin' your time about it."

P.J. chuckled and pulled the car into traffic. "Okay, tell me what you know about our first suspect, Melissa Matthews."

"Well, now, according to Stayle's records, she's an actress on the rise in Hollywood—primarily science-fiction movies."

P.J. nodded. As part of her market research, she kept close tabs on all the major publications, and Melissa Matthews had started to figure prominently in them. It had made it easier to persuade the actress to let P.J. interview her for this story. "Your sister keeps records on her customers? Isn't that a bit unusual?"

"No, she only keeps records on the customers who order custom-made shoes. In order to fit the shoes to their personality, Stayle has to know a bit more about them, y'see. She uses a sophisticated personality test that reveals more than the subject realizes, along with a bit of glamarye to ensure they answer truthfully."

"That's convenient. So, what do we know about Melissa, besides the fact that she's blond and beautiful?"

"Is she, now?" Connor said noncommittally. If P.J. had been hoping for a reaction, it was obvious she wasn't going to get it.

He paused in thought. "Stayle's records show that Melissa is ambitious and hardworking with a definite talent for actin'. That's what Stayle enhanced in the shoes. It'll be interesting to see how she designed them to reflect that."

"Don't you see your sister's designs?"

"Not usually—I'm just the silent partner. She has me handlin' the business end so she can concentrate on the artistic side."

P.J. could understand that—she did essentially the same thing for her family. It wasn't easy acting as the anchor for a bunch of creative head-in-the-clouds types.

She pulled up in front of Melissa's condo, and while Connor slowly unfolded himself from her car, P.J. reached into the back seat for her briefcase.

They walked up the short path and rang the doorbell. Soon, a maid greeted them and ushered them into a spacious living room, furnished all in white.

P.J. set her briefcase down on the glass-topped coffee table and clicked it open, removing her notepad. She stopped, suddenly struck by a thought. "I forgot to ask, what if she *is* the one who stole the shoehorn?"

"If she's handled it recently, the magic will identify itself to me as soon as I shake her hand. Once I know that, I'll worry about how to get it back."

A rustling noise halted their conversation, and P.J. glanced around nervously. Had they been overheard?

"Hello," came a throaty voice from above.

P.J. and Connor turned toward the stairs as Melissa Matthews paused on the landing. She wore a dramatic white jumpsuit with a plunging V neckline that showed off her remarkable tan and her considerable curves.

P.J. and Connor rose to meet her, and Melissa's mouth curved in a cool smile. She strolled down the rest of the stairs, and Connor returned her smile, appearing suitably impressed. P.J. couldn't help but feel a small stab of jealousy. How could anyone compete with a woman who looked like that?

Glancing briefly at P.J., Melissa said, "Ms. Sheridan?" At P.J.'s nod, Melissa turned her gaze back to Connor. "You didn't mention an associate. Who's this?"

P.J. hesitated. She couldn't give Connor's real last name. Melissa might recognize it was the same as Stayle's. "This is my photographer, Connor—"

"Connor Michaels," he interrupted.

Good—he'd chosen one she could remember. P.J. knew from her research that Michael was his middle name.

Connor took a step toward Melissa as if to help her down those last few steps. Irrationally annoyed, P.J. pushed between the two of them. "Connor, why don't you get a picture of her on the stairs?"

"There will be plenty of time for that later," Melissa said, and gestured gracefully toward the living room. "Please, won't you have a seat?"

As P.J. followed Melissa, she met Connor's questioning look and shrugged apologetically, hoping to pass it off as a momentary aberration. How else could she explain it without looking like a jealous shrew?

They all seated themselves, and Melissa glanced around the room. "Neil? Neil, darling, are you here?"

A man appeared from just beyond an open doorway, holding several drink glasses in his hands. Neil "darling" was perhaps fifteen years older than P.J.'s twenty-five, with sandy brown hair and an engaging smile.

"Neil," Melissa said, "this is the reporter I told you about. P. J. Sheridan and her photographer, Connor Michaels." She turned back to P.J. "This is Neil Chalmers, my producer."

Neil smiled and waved the glasses at them. "Welcome. Would you like something to drink?"

"The usual," Melissa replied. Both Connor and P.J. declined.

Neil moved to the bar in the corner of the room to fix the drinks, and Melissa turned to them. "Now, Ms. Sheridan, what would you like to know?"

"As I explained on the phone, I'm here to do a story on the Something Extra boutique," she explained. "I understand you recently ordered a pair of their custom-made shoes?"

Melissa raised one elegantly shod foot. "Yes, aren't they marvelous?"

The high-heeled white sandals were barely held on Melissa's feet with one wide strip across her toes and thin straps of gold-tipped white leather that crisscrossed her slender ankles. They reminded P.J. of the shoes her Barbie doll used to wear, only Melissa's had a clear acrylic heel containing a liquid that glittered with drifting stardust with her every move. On anyone else they would've looked gaudy. On Melissa they gave the impression she was competent and sure of herself.

"Yes, they're wonderful," P.J. said, meaning it. But did they have magic?

True, P.J. did get the impression Melissa was a proficient actress, but was that a result of magic or just Melissa's own considerable presence? There was no way to tell, but P.J. had to believe it was the latter.

As Connor started photographing the actress, P.J. leaned forward. "Something Extra advertises there's magic in these shoes, to enhance their owner's personality. Do you believe that?"

Melissa laughed softly. "I don't know if they're magic or not—I've only had them a few days. All I know is that I feel good when I wear them. Neil says they can't help but enhance my natural personality." She smiled up at Connor as he moved in for a close shot of her face.

P.J. frowned. It was Melissa's feet he was supposed to be interested in.

Neil moved in to hand Melissa her drink and sat down. Connor continued shooting, but Neil ignored him. The producer seemed content to merely observe the conversation, rather than join it.

"So what attracted you to the shoes in the first place?" P.J. asked.

Melissa shrugged. "It was Neil's idea. He'd heard about them at a party in Hollywood and persuaded me to see them since he was coming here to ski, anyway. I fell in love with them. And they're so wonderfully whimsical, I wanted to be one of the first to get a pair of unique, one-of-a-kind Stayle O'Flaherty shoes."

P.J. continued to ask questions about the shoes, and eventually allowed Melissa to steer the conversation back to her career and her upcoming film. Sensing a possible sale to the celebrity fan magazines, P.J. asked, "What's the film about?"

"Oh, it's a wonderful fantasy, something along the lines of *Romancing the Stone,* but with a decidedly Tolkien feel to it—with elves and dragons. Neil is producing it," Melissa said, and smiled fondly at him. "He's going to do for magic-and-fantasy films what Spielberg did for science fiction."

P.J. glanced at Neil and watched his eyes take on an acquisitive gleam.

"Well," he said with an obvious sense of false modesty, "that remains to be seen." He gave P.J. an appreciative glance. "Melissa plays the faerie princess, but there's a part for a lovely elf queen, too. Your looks are exactly what I need. Have you done any acting?"

"No, I've never been interested in acting."

She risked a glance at Connor. Just as she expected, he was grinning wickedly at the thought of her playing one of the faerie folk.

Neil persisted. "You'd be perfect for the part. Perhaps—"

"No," P.J. interrupted. "I'm not interested." She shuddered at the thought of the damage that kind of thing could do to her professional reputation.

Connor rescued her. "If you're finished with the interview, could I get some pictures of Melissa outside?"

P.J. jumped up. "That's a wonderful idea—get some pictures of Melissa *and* her shoes against the mountains."

Melissa rose gracefully and moved toward the sliding glass door. "There's a wonderful view here, outside on the balcony."

Connor and P.J. followed her outside, and Melissa struck an elegant pose against the rustic railing. "How's this?" she asked.

P.J. knew Melissa wasn't trying to seduce Connor, but the actress was so stunning, she just couldn't help but look seductive and alluring.

"Perfect," he agreed. He began snapping pictures furiously, encouraging Melissa to loosen up as P.J. watched in tight-lipped silence.

When he paused to change the film, Melissa smiled at Connor. "Can we take a break now? I'm a little thirsty."

"Good idea," Connor said, and glanced at P.J. "Would you mind getting her a drink?"

P.J. didn't know how to refuse without appearing boorish, so she nodded curtly and went in to fetch one.

As she slid the door shut, P.J. heard Connor's low voice and Melissa's tinkling laugh. P.J. snorted in disgust and moved swiftly inside. Neil sat in the spot P.J. had recently vacated, running a cloth over the table.

"Sorry," he said. "I'm afraid I spilled Melissa's drink and got some of your papers wet. I was just trying to wipe them off." He shrugged apologetically.

"Don't worry about it. They'll dry and I've got everything on disk, anyway." There was less than an inch of liquid left in the glass. Good enough. P.J. scooped it up and hurried back outside.

Melissa peered over Connor's shoulder where he sat changing the film. Connor glanced up and grinned at the actress with a gleam in his eye.

"Here's your drink," P.J. blurted out.

Melissa turned to face her and smiled. "Thank you," she said, accepting the glass.

P.J. frowned. "Are you finished here, Connor?" she snapped. "We have a trip to pack for."

"Yes, we're finished," he said, and packed the film and camera inside his bag.

Back inside, P.J. shook Melissa's hand. "Thank you for the interview. I'll send you a copy when it's published."

Melissa thanked her and turned to Connor, who held her hand for what seemed like an inordinate amount of time.

P.J. gave him a sidelong glance. Was he working his so-called magic on Melissa now, to see if she had the talisman? If so, P.J. couldn't see any visible signs of it. Nothing, that is, but the obvious magic his considerable masculine presence was having on the actress. P.J. knew that magic well.

Connor glanced at P.J. and gave a small shake of his head. Okay, so Melissa wasn't the thief. Or at least Connor hadn't fingered her as the thief. Why didn't that surprise P.J.?

"And what about the pictures?" Melissa asked. "Will I get copies of those, as well?"

Connor gave Melissa one of those heart-stopping smiles that P.J. had come to think of as hers alone. "I'll be happy to give you copies," he said.

They said their goodbyes and Neil waved his farewell from behind the bar. "So long, folks. And remember, P.J., if you ever change your mind, just look me up. I'm in the book."

P.J. nodded curtly and headed out the door behind Connor. As he folded himself into her car, he said, "He's wrong, y'know."

Annoyed, she snapped, "Wrong? Wrong about what?"

Connor chuckled. "Oh, you look nothin' like an elf. Elfin women are slight creatures, flat as a board, with sharp features and silver hair." His gaze raked her. "And while you're slight, you've got curves in all the right places."

"But not as many curves as Melissa," she said flatly, daring him to disagree.

"Perhaps not, but yours is a warm, passionate beauty, whilst hers is cool and aloof."

P.J.'s mouth dropped open in astonishment as she took in his lazy smile. Just when she thought she'd gotten good and mad at the handsome hunk, he had to go and say something really nice. If he kept this up, she'd fall for him soon—and hard.

She clammed up for the rest of the ride, not wanting to let him know how much he affected her. When she dropped him off at the Vail Village parking lot, he leaned down next to her car window. "I'll not be wishing to put myself inside this torture chamber again, so I'll be picking you up tomorrow for our trip. What time was it, now?" He lightly stroked her cheek with one finger, sending her insides fluttering again.

"Oh, yes. Just a moment." Flustered, P.J. reached into the back and pulled her briefcase into the passenger seat. "I made you a copy of the itinerary. It's a little damp, but you can still read it."

Connor accepted the paper and scanned it. "Thanks. Well, I'll be picking you up at eight, then."

P.J. glanced down to check her copy of the itinerary, but it wasn't there. No matter, she could print out another one. "I'll be ready," she promised, and started the car.

He waved goodbye and she eased into traffic, resisting the urge to glance back for another look. He's off-limits, she reminded herself. Not only was he her employer, but he still thought himself a leprechaun.

Of course, if he really was a leprechaun, that was another matter entirely.... Her heart leapt in hope, but her logical mind discarded the possibility. What were the odds of that?

THE NEXT MORNING, Connor parked in front of P.J.'s house and got out of the car. Before he could even make it to the sidewalk, he spotted P.J. hurrying out the door, lugging a large suitcase in one hand and her briefcase in the other.

"Here, let me take that," he chided.

He swung her suitcase on top of his in the trunk and opened the door for her. He tried to catch her eye, but she avoided his gaze. Ah, no, he couldn't have that. Softly he said, "You look nice today, lass."

P.J. looked up then, with surprise on her face. "Thank you."

She looked more than nice—she looked feminine and alluring. The soft outlines of a furry pink sweater over a pair of form-fitting burgundy pants faithfully revealed her gentle curves.

Connor sighed inwardly. This woman was mortal—he had no business imagining how those curves would feel molded to his body, nor how she would look with passion warming her cheeks and lighting her eyes. He settled in the car, forcibly reminding himself he couldn't get serious about a woman unless she had faerie blood flowing through her veins.

As they drove off, P.J. asked, "Why the airport at Eagle? I thought that was only for private planes."

"Aye, but 'tis a mite bit closer than Denver."

"But isn't that rather expensive? In terms of your magic, I mean."

"Well, it would be if I had the payin' of it, but the plane actually belongs to my cousin Sean."

"He doesn't mind you borrowing it like this?"

"No, y'see, we faerie folk have established an international bartering network to exchange goods and services. That way we can get what we need by tradin' without having to use up our own gold or magic."

"But borrowing a plane surely isn't comparable to making a pair of shoes."

"Ah, but did you see the price of our shoes, lass?"

P.J. gave him a censorious look and Connor chuckled. She was great fun to tease. "No, lass, my contribution is as leader of the Fae. They reimburse me for administering justice and such. Besides, Sean is piloting the plane. He doesn't mind—our family is a large one, spread all over the world, and he enjoys visitin' them."

"I see. So, tell me, what's our next suspect like?"

"Steadman Jarvis is a stockbroker. Stayle's records show he's a slippery, cunning one, too. I'm bettin' on him to be the thief."

Sudden disappointment stabbed through him at the thought. If Jarvis was the thief, would P.J. forgo the rest of the trip and the interviews? Connor almost hoped the man would be innocent, so Connor could spend more time getting to know her better.

He parked at the tiny airport and took the luggage out to the airplane. When Sean spotted them, he straightened his rangy form, his eyes widening as he spotted P.J.

His cousin's overt appreciation generated instant feelings of possessiveness and protectiveness in Connor's breast. Connor gave Sean a warning look, informing him in no uncertain terms that P.J. was off-limits. Sean grinned and raised his arms in a hands-off gesture, backing away. To emphasize his point, Connor placed a hand on the small of P.J.'s back to assist her up the narrow steps into the plane.

She stiffened at his touch. Gone was the warm, inviting woman of their dinner date. Instead, he was stuck with the hard-bitten reporter who'd evidently decided to have none of Connor O'Flaherty.

The thought disturbed him more than he'd expected, kindling to life an instant challenge. Unfortunately none of the O'Flahertys had ever been able to resist a challenge.

And though it went against everything he believed in, Connor had the urgent desire to make love to this mortal, to continue what they'd started at the covered bridge and have her soft and yielding in his arms again.

He eyed her speculatively as she took her seat. Of course he couldn't get serious about her, but if he made his intentions clear up front, maybe they could enjoy a warm, intimate interlude with no strings attached.

Aye, that would be the tough part—keeping her from attaching strings to his heart.

Chapter Five

After a comfortable night in a well-appointed New York hotel, Connor went downstairs to meet P.J. in the restaurant. When he spotted her he grinned, and she smiled back hesitantly with a murmured "Good morning," then returned to perusing her menu.

Connor frowned. Today he wasn't going to let her get away with that. Today he was going to rediscover the warm, responsive woman he'd found at the covered bridge.

Connor glanced at the hovering waitress. "No coffee, thank you, and none for the lady, either." He shared a smile with P.J., subtly reminding her they did have some things in common.

They placed their breakfast orders and his smile grew warmer. "And how did you sleep last night, lass?" A caressing note crept into his voice at the thought of how she must look in bed. Curled up like a kitten, he'd bet, with her soft pink lips slightly parted and all that lovely long dark hair loose and swirling about her creamy white shoulders.

His thoughts must have been evident, for a faint blush stained her cheeks, complementing the maroon of her jacket. "I slept fine, thank you. And you?"

Connor grinned. He liked to see the very professional P.J. blush, make her aware of him as a man, no matter how hard she tried not to be. He ignored her wary look. She was obviously expecting him to come back with an innuendo, so he'd surprise her. "Not bad. 'Tis an advantage havin' connections in the hotel business. They know what a big behemoth I am, so they keep a few extralong beds around for people like me."

P.J. visibly relaxed. "I imagine that would be difficult." She cast a furtive glance around the dining room and lowered her voice. With a slight tinge of embarrassment, she said, "Are all of your... connections leprechauns?"

"No, though they are all Fae. Most of the old legends have a bit of truth to them, and different types of Fae have an affinity for certain types of professions. For example, the owners of this hotel have more than a touch of the domestic hob in them."

She compressed her lips into a thin line and raised one eyebrow. Connor was beginning to understand that look. It meant he'd just said something she found preposterous, but was too polite to challenge him. "I thought hobs worked only for milk left on the hearth overnight."

He couldn't help but chuckle. So she'd been reading up on the legends, had she? "They used to, but 'tis mighty hard to raise a family or get anywhere in life if you're paid in nothing but milk!"

She chuckled along with him as the waitress brought their breakfasts. Connor continued, encouraged by P.J.'s relaxed mood. "'Twas one of the reasons the faerie folk joined forces—our kind was dyin' out fast, and we needed to find a way to keep the mortals from dilutin' our blood further or runnin' us off the land out of sheer ignorance. So we banded together to share our strengths."

P.J. nodded in comprehension, but her expression turned serious again. Ah, no, he couldn't have that. Casually he stroked the back of her hand, wanting her to notice *him,* not just his words.

She blushed a lovely rose color and drew her hand away under the guise of reaching for a piece of toast. Connor grinned as she determinedly changed the subject.

"You keep talking about mortal blood diluting your race. Just how much faerie blood must you have to be considered Fae, anyway?"

He shrugged. "'Tisn't really how much blood you have so much as how much power you can raise. They are related, though. Being one-eighth faerie gives you a measure of power you can use, but when it gets down to one-sixteenth you lose a lot. Bein' one-sixteenth leprechaun, for instance, just makes you a wee bit luckier than other mortals when it comes to dealing with gold or money, especially if you've managed to key a talisman. I'm almost full faerie, and I'm *very* lucky," he said, unable to suppress a wicked grin. "I met you, didn't I?"

Ignoring his verbal sally, P.J. said, "Only leprechauns have talismans to focus the magic?"

"No, lass, the others use whatever seems more appropriate for their particular talent. Most faerie folk have an affinity for gold, but only we leprechauns have the ability to use it to wield our power. 'Tis why you find us so often as leaders of the little people."

Her gaze turned distant again. "I see." She glanced at her watch and pulled her briefcase onto her lap.

Saints, but she was hard to reach this morning. Connor sighed and gave up—for the moment. "I guess 'tis almost time to be leavin' for our meeting with Steadman Jarvis." He reached into his breast pocket to pull out Stayle's notes. "I've his profile here—"

P.J. frowned. "No, wait. I don't think that's such a good idea. If I'm to write a story about how well your sister's shoes enhance people's personalities, I'd prefer to make my own judgments first, then compare them to her notes."

P.J. searched through her briefcase. "Darn," she muttered. "I must have left my pen at home."

She looked uncharacteristically upset about the loss of a pen. "'Tisn't the end of the world, y'know. I have one you can borrow, lass." He offered her his gold pen.

She took it. "Thanks. It's just that I've had that silver pen since my first assignment. It's brought me luck on every story I've covered so far. I know it's silly, but it's kind of my good-luck charm, like a—" She stopped, a stricken look in her eyes.

He grinned. "Like a talisman?"

"Yeah, I guess." She avoided his gaze as she scribbled a few notes on her pad, then handed the pen back to him.

"That's all right, lass. We've yet to find one of the Fae who use silver in their talisman," he teased her. He gestured dismissively. "You can keep the pen if you'll be needin' it."

She rubbed her hand on her skirt. "No, thanks. All that gold makes my hand itch like crazy. I'm sure I've got a pencil somewhere in my purse—that'll do for now."

Itching, allergies—where had he heard that before? And why did it seem so important? Connor thought hard for a moment, but the memory eluded him, so he shook his head and turned back to the task at hand. "All right, then, shall we go?"

He laid a couple of bills on the table and followed P.J. out the door, slinging his camera case over his shoulder. They rode a taxi to the high-rise building where Jarvis worked and took the elevator to one of the top floors. Approaching the receptionist, P.J. said, "We have an appointment with Mr. Jarvis. Is he in?"

The receptionist nodded toward a group of people clustered around a young man who was telling a convoluted story that involved much hand waving, accompanied by bursts of laughter from the admiring crowd. "Yes, that's him," she said flatly, clearly unimpressed. "The one in the middle."

Connor watched as Steadman Jarvis continued his story. Young, handsome, with his hair precision cut in the latest style, Jarvis plainly had the crowd enthralled and the world at his feet. Speaking of feet...had Jarvis worn Stayle's shoes as P.J. requested? Connor glanced down when a gap in the crowd appeared.

Yes, he had. The shoes were a deep rich brown of the finest leather, the welt and eyelets ostentatiously trimmed in what had to be pure gold. Saints, even the shoelaces were tipped in little gold dollar signs.

How vulgar. Had Stayle really designed these shoes? They did have her distinctive flair, but what had she been thinking?

Connor concentrated on Jarvis, trying to see him as the shoes projected him. Stilling his mind, Connor let the shoes' magic take hold. He received a strong image of a ruthless young entrepreneurial genius—a man well on his way up the ladder of success who wouldn't worry about how he got there. A man who'd lie and cheat his own grandmother if he thought it would make him an extra buck.

Amused, Connor realized Stayle had kept her customer agreement to the letter. She'd enhanced his natural personality all right, and obviously played up on what he thought was important—his ruthless success. To others like him, the shoes would project an attitude they wanted to emulate. To those honest folks Steadman Jarvis sought to cheat, they would see him for what he really was—a weasel. Stayle had outdone herself on this one.

Curious as to P.J.'s reaction, he glanced down at her. She watched Jarvis with an apprehensive frown on her face, much as a minnow would watch a shark. Good. Stayle's magic was working.

Jarvis's story came to an end when he spotted them. He left his group of admirers, saying, "The press, you know." He took a good look at P.J., then smoothed his hair and straightened his tie. He strutted over, oozing self-confidence.

Holding out his hand, he said, "Ms. Sheridan, I presume? May I call you P.J.?"

"Certainly," P.J. said as she clasped the man's hand. She didn't seem to enjoy the sensation and drew back quickly, though Jarvis seemed inclined to linger.

She gestured toward Connor. "And this is my photographer, Connor...Michaels."

Connor held out his hand in anticipation, but Jarvis had already turned back to P.J. and was escorting her into the office, his head bent attentively toward hers and his hand against the small of her back. Annoyed, Connor just sighed and followed them into the office. He'd just have to find an excuse to touch the man's hand later.

Jarvis waved Connor and P.J. to guest chairs before seating himself at his high-tech Plexiglas desk, with a magnificent view of the city behind him. Connor noted with amusement that Jarvis's chair was raised about six inches higher than theirs. *Faith, he doesn't miss a trick, does he?*

Jarvis leaned back, steepled his fingers in front of his face and gave them a toothy smile. "So, what did you want to know?"

P.J. pulled out her notepad and pencil. "As I said on the phone, I'm doing a story on Something Extra and the famous people who shop there."

Connor hid a grin. P.J. had certainly caught this guy's measure, all right. She knew just how to play him.

"So," she continued. "I understand you had a pair of shoes especially made to fit your personality. Can you tell me why?"

"Of course. I specialize in finding unique securities for my clients—stocks that are little known but have a high potential for growth. When I received the prospectus on Something Extra, it looked too good to be true, so I took a look for myself."

"Too good to be true?"

"Yes, the high concept was intriguing—an upscale shoe boutique catering to the very rich has a certain appeal."

Yeah, snob appeal. Though, to be fair, it was also designed to appeal to anyone with faerie blood. Connor grimaced. It was obvious which category Jarvis fell into—he was just the type to steal a faerie's shoehorn.

Jarvis gestured enthusiastically. "My guess is it's going to be one of the hottest properties in the near future, and my guesses are seldom wrong."

He went on at length, painting a glowing picture of the boutique's prospects and his own brilliance in discovering it. Connor wondered when P.J. was going to shut him up, but she just let him talk, nodding every once in a while. Bored, Connor decided to start acting like a photographer. He moved around the room, snapping the man's picture at various angles.

Jarvis became more expansive, leaping to his feet and gesturing dramatically with his hands, playing to the camera. "And the best part is, I learned that Connor O'Flaherty is one of the partners." A look of surprise crossed his face. "Hey, big guy," he said as he lightly punched Connor in the arm. "You two have the same first name. Bet you wish you had his talents, too, huh?"

Connor just grunted noncommittally and squinted through the camera to see P.J.'s reaction. She had an arrested look on her face. "Oh? Who's this O'Flaherty?"

"He used to be a Wall Street whiz kid—one of the best mutual-fund managers ever. Managed a whole family of funds, but primarily specialized in gold securities and unique corporations like this one."

"Used to?" she queried.

"Yeah, I guess he burned out or something. Happens to the best of us, you know," he said with cocky self-assurance, implying it would never happen to him. "I figure if he's in on it, it's gotta be good."

"I see," P.J. said, and gave Connor a speculative look. Uh-oh, it looked like he was in for a grilling later. "So, I understand why you'd want to check out the company. But what made you decide to buy a pair of their custom-made 'magic' shoes?"

He glanced down at his shoes. "Dunno, really. I guess because they're a great conversation piece—a real one-of-a-kind item. No one else will ever have a pair like these. I kinda like that idea."

"And the magic? What about that?"

He grinned. "Oh, I'm not saying they've got the real stuff, but they've sure worked magic for me. It's strange, but I've been totally honest with my customers—not that I wasn't before, you understand," he added hastily. "But I've been more forthcoming than I strictly need to be and it's really paid off. My accounts are doing great, I'm getting more respect and I've been given this great corner office. It probably would've happened anyway—" he sat down and placed his feet on the desk, with his hands behind his head "—but just in case, I'm not taking these babies off!"

Connor captured his pose on film—the consummate self-indulgent snob.

Irritated, Connor straightened, then thanked the man for his time, holding his hand out. Jarvis had to either take it and ruin his pretty pose or look like a jerk in front of P.J. Jarvis frowned, but did the polite thing and reached to shake Connor's hand.

Ah, the moment he'd been waiting for. Connor grinned in triumph as he clasped Jarvis's hand firmly and pressed his talisman ring against the man's fingers.

His grin faded. The man's handshake was firm and quick, but unfortunately devoid of any trace of magic. At P.J.'s questioning look, Connor shook his head in disappointment. No, Jarvis wasn't the one.

P.J. nodded, then wrapped up the interview and finally took her leave.

Connor followed dutifully behind, trying to give the impression of the dull but faithful photographer and wondering how long it would take the inquisitive P.J. to start ferreting out his past. Surprisingly, she asked a wholly unrelated question as he hailed a cab.

"Didn't you say Stayle added more glamarye to make her less honest clients turn to 'the direction of the right'?"

"Aye, that I did."

"Then what about Jarvis? Why'd the magic help him? He seemed like a real sleazeball if ever I've seen one."

They entered the taxi and Connor gave the driver the address of their hotel. "Aye, he is that, but give the magic a chance, lass. It's only had a week or so to work on him. And remember, it only rewards him when he does the right thing—when he helps people instead of trying to cheat them."

"So he'll turn into a good, honest mutual-fund manager someday?"

Connor nodded.

"Like you were?"

Ah, finally, the question he'd been waiting for. "So, lass, are you a wee bit miffed at me?" He couldn't help but stroke the softness of her cheek as he smiled down into her beautiful dark eyes.

She gave him a half smile. "No, I'm not miffed at you. Not even a 'wee' bit. I'm just surprised, that's all. I'm sure you know I did a little research on your background."

Connor nodded. And his sources told him she'd concentrated on his police and medical records. Nothing there would have led her to his experience on Wall Street.

P.J. shrugged. "I guess I just didn't delve deep enough. So, were you as successful as he says?"

It was Connor's turn to shrug. "Aye, that I was."

"So why'd you quit? Burnout?"

She appeared genuinely interested. Not sarcastic or biting—just interested. "Not really. I just got tired of the city and of sharks like Jarvis. I wanted to go somewhere where making money wasn't the be-all and end-all of existence."

"So instead you moved to Vail, where skiing is the be-all and end-all of existence."

He had to chuckle. "True, but 'tis a harmless pastime and its practitioners rarely hurt anyone but themselves. Besides, I wanted to go back to Colorado, back to wide-open spaces and green hills, as far away from the concentration of cold, cruel iron as possible."

"So that part of the legend's true? You... faeries—" he grinned at the way she struggled with the word "—have an aversion to iron?"

"Yes, but 'tisn't as bad as it used to be. Times were, unadulterated iron would cause us to lose our powers altogether—sometimes our very lives. But now, with all the crossbreedin' with mortals we've done, 'tisn't so bad. And then again, there's powerful little pure iron in the world. 'Tis mostly steel we have problems with."

He raised his hand to stroke her cheek again, and P.J. blushed, lowering her eyes. "Oh? Uh, what kind of problems?"

He shot her an apprehensive glance. "You'll not be puttin' this in the article, will you? I'd hate to have one of my people brought low on account of my waggin' tongue."

She eyed him thoughtfully. "No, I promise I won't print that."

He nodded. If she said she wouldn't print it, she wouldn't. "It doesn't hurt us anymore, but too high a concentration of it causes our powers to weaken. And 'tis mighty difficult to put a proper spell on something with a lot of iron in it. 'Tisn't worth the trouble."

Their conversation ceased then, for they'd reached the hotel. He followed her into the lobby. "Well, now, lass, our flight to Paris doesn't leave until tomorrow, so what do you say we tour the Big Apple? You've never been here before, have you?''

''No,'' she replied hesitantly. ''I haven't. If it isn't too much trouble, I'd love to do some sight-seeing.''

Connor leaned across her to push the elevator button, smiling down at the excited look in her eyes. The action brought him close to her, so close he could feel the heat from her body and smell her distinct fragrance, a tangy citruslike scent.

He stayed in that position, close to her, and watched her become flustered, avoiding his gaze. He smiled slowly. ''No, lass. 'Tisn't any trouble. 'Tisn't any trouble at all.''

She glanced up with a questioning look that revealed she was as aware of him as he was of her. She licked her lips, and he leaned down closer to their moist invitation. Saints, he couldn't resist her like this.

When she didn't move away, he touched his lips to hers, gently so as not to scare her off. It was just as he remembered—incredibly sweet, yet charged with a potent sensuality that knocked his socks off.

She returned the kiss eagerly and he buried his hands in the silky fall of her long black hair, cradling her head in his hands. She responded with a wondrous, magical kiss that threatened to steal his very soul. It wasn't until P.J. grasped his shirtfront tightly and made a soft noise in her throat that he came to his senses. He pulled back to see if he was going too fast for her, and the trust and naked yearning he saw in her eyes made his pulse leap.

She shuttered her gaze quickly, but not before he caught a faint flash of fear. ''Oh, lass,'' he breathed. He would never hurt her.

"Well, hello there, P.J.," a jovial male voice intruded.

Connor scowled and looked around to see who had accosted them.

P.J. blushed, then pushed away from him, straightening her hair. "Neil, Neil Chalmers, isn't it? What a strange coincidence—we didn't expect to see you here." She extended her hand to shake his, but he just shrugged apologetically as he stood there with his hands full, a briefcase in one hand and an overnight bag in the other.

The elevator opened then, and they all entered. Connor glowered at the interloper, but Neil ignored him. He just continued talking blithely away, as if he and P.J. were the best of friends. "It's not so odd—I have film interests on both coasts. But how marvelous to see someone here I know. Do you have plans for dinner yet?"

"Yes," Connor said shortly, not wanting to spend any more time with this rude lout. Couldn't he see he was intruding?

P.J. gave Connor a censorious glance. "We were just going out sight-seeing, but we hadn't made any plans for dinner yet."

"Great! Then we can all go together. I know of a new restaurant—it's the latest thing. The theater crowd goes there for dinner and I'll introduce you to some of the celebrities. How about it?"

Connor sensed P.J.'s hesitation. Saints, why was she even considering spending any time in this man's company?

"All right," she said, and avoided Connor's gaze.

Neil bounced on his toes, grinning. "Terrif! I'll meet you in the lobby at eight, all right?" He waved goodbye with his briefcase as he got off on his floor.

Connor smiled as the door closed, hiding Neil's smirking face. "Do you really want to be eatin' dinner with that man?" Connor inquired incredulously.

P.J. avoided his gaze. "No, but he looked so lonely, so eager for company, I couldn't turn him down. Besides, the invitation was for both of us, you know, and...I might be able to pick up a couple of tidbits to sell to a gossip magazine."

It was a thin excuse. Connor stared at her searchingly as she opened her door and entered her room.

"It'll only take me a few minutes to change," she said. "I'll be right out."

Connor nodded and waited in the hallway. So, she was a wee bit reluctant to be alone with him, eh? She'd conceded the necessity so far, but she was probably remembering the last time they'd had dinner alone together and how she'd turned all soft and romantic in his arms. Connor smiled in remembrance. Aye, he'd been remembering it, too, and had hoped to repeat the experience.

The devil take Neil Chalmers and his dinner invitation! Connor would just have to do the best he could with the day he had left.

THEY PAINTED the Big Apple green—emerald green— from the top of the Empire State Building, down to the depths of the subway, and all over Times Square. Throughout it all, Connor was both charmed and amused by the excitement and wonder on P.J.'s face as she met each new experience head-on. It was a delight to be with her.

Through her eyes, New York took on a mystical charm, one he'd long since forgotten. They laughed together over silly things and P.J. turned playful, squirting him with mustard when they stopped for one of New York's famous hot dogs, then cavorting in a fountain like a child when he tried to wash it off. Delighted by her whimsical, impish streak, Connor vowed to learn as much about her as he could. Though their relationship couldn't go any further and he knew it was wrong, he just couldn't help himself. He was drawn to her like a pixie to mischief.

As they headed back toward the hotel in a cab, tired but content, Connor put his arm around P.J. and snuggled her close. "So, did you see all you wanted to, lass?"

She smiled up at him. "Yes, thank you, it was wonderful. I just wish..."

She looked so wistful that he wanted to call down the moon and stars for her, anything to see that happy, contented look on her face again. He squeezed her hand. "What, lass? What d'you wish?" he asked gently.

"I wish..." She glanced down at his hand where it covered hers, his ring gleaming. Her gaze turned stony. "Oh, nothing." She pulled out of his embrace and began to root through her handbag. "I know I have lipstick in here somewhere."

Connor wasn't fooled. P.J. wasn't looking for lipstick—she was looking for an excuse to avoid him. Her emotions showed plainly on her face, and when she'd spotted his ring, it was obvious she'd remembered who and what he was. And just as plainly, she still thought he was one brick short of a load.

Irritation filled him. Suddenly it became imperative that she believe in him, that she trust him enough to know he wouldn't lie to her. "You wish I really was magic, don't you, lass?" he said quietly enough so the cabdriver couldn't hear.

P.J. looked up, startled. A wry grin crossed her face. "Are you *sure* you're not a mind reader?"

He caressed her cheek with his fingers. "No, lass. I read your face, not your mind."

A look of comical dismay crossed her features, but she tried hard to control it.

"No, don't. Don't put on your reporter's stone face for me. 'Tis delightful seeing your emotions cross your face. It's as one with your honesty, and I appreciate that." He smiled down at her. "I have a wish, too, y'know. I wish you'd believe in me—trust me enough to know I'm not lying to you."

Her expressive features settled into distress. "I wish I could, too, but you haven't done anything to prove it. And I'm sorry, but I must have proof. I've searched too long and hard for real magic to merely take it on faith."

"What about the shoes? Didn't they convince you?"

She shook her head. "No, they're marvelous and quite apt at describing their owners' personalities, but that doesn't mean they're magic. I need concrete proof—something that can't be explained by coincidence or trickery."

Connor sighed. He hated using his power for parlor tricks, but if that's what would convince her and keep her on the case, then so be it. He wasn't squandering his magic, he assured himself, he was using it in a good cause—to get Stayle's talisman back. "All right, lass, I guess I can afford to use a little magic. I'll just cast a glamour over something to make it appear something it isn't. Nothing big, mind you. I don't want to use much of it. Would that convince you?"

P.J. looked doubtful. "Maybe."

"All right, then, you name it. Tell me what seeming you'd like me to cast. Just don't make it anything too strange—we wouldn't want to alarm anyone."

They came to a stop at a red light and P.J. pointed to the street corner. "There," she said. "Make that phone booth disappear."

That was easy enough. Connor concentrated, focusing his power. He felt the slight mental pressure that signaled the presence of his magic and released a tiny jolt of it through his ring. Not too much, just enough to do the job. His finger tingled as the ring released the power.

He crossed his eyes in an old faerie trick, so he could see the glamarye in action. Yes, it worked. He could still see the phone booth with his true sight, but to every mortal around it had disappeared. As he watched, an unwary pedestrian walked smack into it. Hastily he restored it to normal.

He turned to P.J. and grinned. "Well?"

P.J. glanced askance at him. "Well, what?"

"Well, I made it disappear like you asked, didn't I?"

She gave him a pitying look. "No, Connor, it didn't disappear."

"Are you daft, woman? The blamed thing vanished, just as you asked. Didn't you see the man walk into it?"

"Yes, I saw him walk into it, but what does that prove?"

"It proves he couldn't see it, because 'twas invisible!"

P.J. looked disappointed and more than a little angry. "It proves no such thing. That was pure coincidence."

Frustrated beyond endurance, Connor constructed an illusion she couldn't ignore. A grinning jester popped out of the back of the driver's seat, bobbing like a deranged jack-in-the-box as it shoved its face into hers, crossed its eyes and blew a raspberry, then vanished.

P.J. didn't even blink.

He gaped at her. "You really can't see my glamarye, can you? Well, that explains it, then. You have true sight." No wonder she was so good at debunking charlatans.

"True sight?" P.J. looked disbelieving and suspicious.

"Yes, all faerie folk have true sight—"

"But we've already established I'm not faerie."

Yes—her allergy to gold precluded that. Saints, but he wished he could remember what it was about allergies that was so important. "Aye, but it also occurs in mortals. 'Tis rare, only one in a hundred thousand mortals have it, and I guess you're one of them. This complicates things."

She raised an eyebrow. "I'll say."

"But I know a way to help you see the illusion, even—"

"No, please," she interrupted in an exasperated tone. "Let's just drop it, okay?"

Connor nodded reluctantly and clenched the armrest in frustration. Now the only thing that would convince her was *real* magic—not the mere illusion of glamarye—and that was just too expensive to waste on frivolous things.

They entered the hotel and Connor kept pace with P.J.'s brisk strides. In a low, frustrated voice, he said, "Can't you just trust me?"

She turned on him. "How can I? I'm sure you believe what you're saying, but if I can't see it, how can I believe? How can I trust you?" She turned back and strode toward the check-in desk.

Connor felt like roaring in frustration. He followed and stood impatiently next to her as she waited for the desk clerk to notice her. Taking a deep breath to calm himself, he said, "Lass—"

"As with all my investigations, I'll give you the benefit of the doubt until you prove your claims one way or the other, but I won't believe blindly." She gave him a stern look. "I can't—my reputation would be in shreds. What could I write? 'He can't prove it, but I know he's a leprechaun'?"

Connor sighed. She was right. He'd just have to find another way to make her trust him and to make her see the magic she was so eager to find.

Raised voices penetrated his reverie. The desk clerk, wearing a long-suffering look on his face, was trying to soothe an incensed hotel customer. Apparently he wasn't very successful. "Well!" the angry matron huffed. "I've stayed in the finest hotels all over the world and this has never happened to me before. I demand to speak to the manager, and the police!"

Connor glanced around. His hob cousin, the manager, was already on his way to take care of the situation. When the manager arrived, the desk clerk turned to them with a sigh of relief, saying, "I'm terribly sorry for the inconvenience. How may I help you?"

"Our keys, please," P.J. said, and gave the clerk their room numbers and identification. Connor could see her inquisitive mind working a mile a minute as she turned a sympathetic smile on the hapless man and said, "What was that all about?"

The clerk gave her a tight smile as he handed her the key and an envelope he'd pulled from her box. "Nothing for you to worry about, ma'am. The guest has a lot of jewels and she refuses to put them in the hotel safe. She very unwisely left her ruby-and-diamond bracelet on the table in her room and went to get some ice. Apparently she left the door ajar, and when she came back the bracelet was gone."

"Really?" P.J. asked. "Do you think I could help—"

Connor retrieved his key and grabbed her arm. "Never mind. I'm sure the manager has the situation well in hand. Now, shall we be making plans for dinner?"

P.J. frowned at him, but acceded. Opening the envelope, she read the note. "Neil's made reservations for us. He'll meet us downstairs at seven."

Connor bowed to the inevitable. Though he wanted to be alone with this wonderful woman, to learn as much as he could about her, now was not the time, not when his attempts at proving himself had fallen so flat.

He dressed for dinner and went downstairs. For once he was the first to show up. A ping announced the arrival of the elevator, and the doors whisked open to reveal a vision he was sure would haunt his dreams.

P.J. stood there, looking absolutely stunning in a short, flame red dress that clung faithfully to every curve of her luscious figure. As she moved gracefully toward him, a slit over her right leg winked open, revealing tantalizing glimpses of her thigh. He reluctantly dragged his gaze from the sight, only to have it snag on the sight of the creamy flesh of her high, firm breasts straining above the low neckline.

She stopped next to him and smiled, her glossy lips parting over even white teeth. Connor's heart turned over and he felt a rush of longing surge through him. Saints, didn't the witch realize what she was doing to him with her innocent smile and her dangerous dress?

He didn't want to share this vision with any man. With any luck he'd be able to spirit her away before Neil showed up. Connor's throat went dry and he took a step toward her.

Answering yearning flickered momentarily in her eyes, but was replaced by a flash of panic. She took a step back, then glanced past him and waved. Connor turned. Damn. It was too late.

Neil grinned back at them. He looked dapper in his evening clothes, the effect slightly spoiled by the white bandage wrapped around his right hand. He waved at them from the elevator, then hurried over.

"Hello, folks. I hope you haven't been waiting long." He held up his bandaged hand ruefully. "I just had a run-in with a paring knife and I lost—sliced my palm good. Shall we go?"

P.J. agreed, looking distinctly relieved.

Ah, so that's how she was playing it—using Neil as a buffer between the two of them. Connor grinned and followed them out the door. Knowing P.J. was more affected than she wanted to let on made the evening's prospects a lot more bearable.

The evening proved to be as boring as he'd expected, but Connor didn't let it show. For the most part he watched silently as Neil chattered on at length about his new film, effectively monopolizing the conversation. And P.J. just encouraged him. She didn't appear to be enjoying herself, either, but she seemed just as reluctant to be alone with Connor.

That touch of panic he'd seen in her eyes had been very telling. He didn't want to do anything to frighten her, and if this was what it took to reassure her...

Neil took another clumsy bite with his bandaged hand. "So, P.J., have you given any thought to appearing as the elf queen in my film?"

"No, I told you before," she answered calmly. "I'm not interested."

"Not interested? How can you not be interested?" Neil asked dramatically. "Everyone wants to be a star."

"Not me," P.J. said simply. "I do better in the background, away from the lights and glitter."

"But you'd be perfect as the elf queen." Neil leaned closer and winked at her. "I've been doing some investigating of my own, and I found out you know quite a bit about these things. If you won't act, can I persuade you to be my magic expert on the film? I need someone to tell me how it's really supposed to work."

P.J. shook her head. "I'm no expert, but you might want to ask Connor."

Neil looked surprised. "Connor? I thought you were just a photographer. Do you have an interest in magic, too?"

The man's surprise and condescension were irritating. "You might say that," Connor conceded. Briefly wrangling with his scruples, he gave in to the impulse to let Neil have a wee taste of that magic.

As Neil reached for his wineglass, Connor touched his ring and sent a tiny surge of power winging along it. He suppressed a smile as the chillingly real illusion formed before him, and Neil's wineglass ignited in a burst of flames.

A passing waiter gasped and dropped his tray, but Neil just took an unconcerned sip of his wine, his lips passing harmlessly through the fire.

Damn, Neil couldn't see the illusion, either. *Two* mortals in one day who had true sight? What were the odds? Connor frowned and made the illusion vanish before he frightened any more innocent victims.

It just wasn't his day.

Chapter Six

P.J. hurried to change her clothes in the charming little French hotel room, feeling excitement and anticipation course through her. Connor was going to show her Paris!

They had the entire day free to explore the city at their leisure. They deserved it, too, after spending the previous day traveling, and the evening before that in the company of the very boring Neil Chalmers.

Boy, what a mistake that had been. She'd only agreed to have dinner with the producer to keep a buffer between herself and Connor, to somehow stop or slow down the pace of their relationship. She was falling too hard, too fast, and it scared her.

The evening hadn't gone at all as she'd planned. By refusing to engage Neil in meaningless conversation, Connor's silence simply played up the differences between the two men. She hadn't been able to keep from comparing Neil's boasting to Connor's quiet competence, Neil's arrogance to Connor's amiability or Neil's slick good looks to Connor's innate sensuality. No matter how she fought it, she'd found herself more and more enmeshed in the magic the big Irishman's presence wove around her.

She sighed. There was no sense fighting it anymore. If it was going to happen, she might as well enjoy it—starting now. P.J. slipped her shoes on and tapped on the connecting door to Connor's room.

He opened the door, glanced at her jeans and sweater and grinned. She couldn't help but laugh. He was wearing the same thing she was, even down to the exact same shade of emerald green in their sweaters. "Everyone will think we're twins," she said with a grin.

His answering smile was soft and sexy. "Nay, lass, not twins. They'll think we're lovers. Paris is made for lovers, y'know."

P.J.'s heart beat a fast rhythm in her chest. Lovers...was that how he thought of them? Part of her hoped so, desperately.

Another part was wary, reminding her there was no future in falling in love with a man who had delusions of being a faerie king. And after what she'd learned yesterday, P.J. figured she had a pretty good idea where those fantasies stemmed from. Despite Connor's protestations to the contrary, his high-stress Wall Street job must have caused a nervous breakdown, and the faerie-king delusion was just one of his lingering symptoms.

Luckily it was a harmless one and would probably disappear once he recovered. P.J. sighed in relief. All she had to do was play along until he finally came to his senses. Maybe she could even subtly help him to see how ridiculous his claims were.

"Lass? Are you all right?" Connor's voice broke into her reverie.

She smiled at him. "I'm fine. Just fine." She grabbed his hand and gave him a slow, sexy smile that made his eyes widen. "Come on, Connor, let's see Paris."

The rest of the day was full of enchantment as they explored the city made for lovers. The weather cooperated, giving them warm, balmy breezes in the midst of a cold October, and even the Parisians' fabled rudeness softened under the warmth and charm of Connor's smile.

They visited the Louvre first, and strolled companionably amid the priceless art treasures. They both enjoyed the impressionists Paris was famous for, but had a hard time appreciating the somber darkness of the old masters.

Connor kept P.J. entertained with amusing speculations as to what the subjects were thinking about as they posed for their portraits. "This one," said Connor as they paused in front of a picture of a corpulent man with a faraway look in his eyes, "is wonderin' when he'll be called to supper, and this one—" a portrait of a pinch-faced debutante "—is sittin' on a pin."

They paused in front of the roped-off section holding the world's most famous painting. P.J. asked, "And Mona Lisa, what about her?"

Connor tilted his head and studied the painting. "Ah, that's easy. Da Vinci had faerie blood, y'know."

"Did he, now?" she mocked.

"Aye, 'tis why his paintings are so grand—he had faerie magic to enhance his talent." The look on Connor's face was earnest, but a twinkle still lurked in his eyes.

"And what is she thinking?"

Connor studied the painting thoughtfully. "She's thinkin' how foolish we are for wanderin' through this musty old building when we could be outside enjoying the beautiful day."

P.J. giggled, earning a stern look from the guard. "Well, she's right. Let's go."

They hurried out of the museum, laughing at the scandalized expressions of the guards and the tourists. Once out in the sunshine, Connor breathed in deeply and threw his arms wide. "Ah, fresh air at last."

P.J. punched his arm playfully. "You have absolutely no culture in your soul."

His look was mournful. "Aye, that I've not." He caught her around the waist and tilted her chin up with one finger. "But you love me anyway, don't you, lass?" His gaze was hooded, his eyes searching as a small smile played around his lips.

Her stomach did somersaults. Love him? No, she wasn't ready for that yet. But how *did* she feel about him? This wonderful man with his ready humor, his tenderness, his lovely Irish lilt . . . his delusions? No, it wasn't love, but she was beginning to care about him more than she should.

"Oh, sure," she said lightly, squirming out of his grasp. "But I'll love you even more if you show me the Eiffel Tower."

The rest of the day took on a magical, dreamlike quality, as if they'd spent the time in a fantasy world.

P.J. stored the sights and sounds in her heart, in a series of vignettes she'd never forget.

Strolling down the Champs-Elysées, feeling cherished when Connor pointed out items of interest and entwined his fingers with hers.

Standing at the top of the Eiffel Tower, gazing raptly over the city spread beneath them, seeing the tenderness in his eyes as he smoothed back a strand of her hair.

Taking in the sights and sounds of Montmartre, and being pulled into the protective circle of Connor's arms when a troop of teenagers roared by on skates. Gazing up at him, feeling safe and warm, celebrating the moment in a tender kiss, then continuing their stroll with arms around each other's waist, hips bumping companionably.

The magic continued until lights began winking on all over the city. Night was falling, and the air turned chilly. Reluctantly they returned to the hotel.

Pausing outside their rooms, P.J. gazed up at Connor with a smile. "Thank you. I had a wonderful day."

Connor flicked her cheek with his finger. "It's not over yet."

Her heart rose into her throat. "No?"

"Nay, lass. I've ordered dinner in my room, in half an hour." He smiled, flashing that dimple she couldn't resist. "I'll be seeing you then."

P.J. nodded wordlessly and slipped into her room. She sighed. The best was yet to come—an intimate dinner for two in Connor's room.

She slipped on a clinging jersey dress in a soft rose pink, deciding not to wear a bra. It would only ruin the lines of the dress, and she loved the sensuous feel of the fabric caressing her breasts—it made her feel wonderfully wicked. She quickly retouched her makeup and dabbed the perfume Connor had bought her behind her ears and between her breasts at the low neckline. Now she was ready for anything.

It had been a long time since she'd felt this way about a man—nervous and excited, and very much aroused. No, come to think of it, she'd never felt this way before. She'd never wanted any other man like she wanted Connor. She only hoped he felt the same way about her.

Connor knocked on their adjoining door, and P.J. wiped her damp palms on a towel before she mustered the courage to answer it. Swallowing hard, she opened the door and her heart skipped a beat. He looked absolutely delicious in a dark dinner suit, damp hair curling at the collar of his crisp white shirt. He gave her a heart-melting smile and escorted her into his room.

A table had been elegantly set for two, the room lit only by the softly flickering candles in the silver candelabra and the city lights twinkling through the window.

It was beautiful, a scene set for seduction. P.J. relaxed and her lips curved into a smile of anticipation. "How lovely. How did you do all this without my hearing it?"

He smiled, then brought her hand to his lips and kissed it softly. "Magic, of course. What did you expect?"

She frowned. She didn't want to be reminded of his illness; it would spoil the mood.

"Not my glamarye," he clarified. "The hotel manager's magic. He had it waiting for me when we got back. All the world loves a lover, and he's no exception."

Lover? Her heart thumped erratically and her knees went weak at the thought of what that implied. Trustingly, she placed her hand in his, and he led her to the elegantly set table and seated her.

P.J. remembered very little of what they ate or talked about, but she could have written chapter and verse on Connor's expression as his smoldering gaze lingered on her low neckline, or the way her breasts tightened at his look and her limbs went warm and boneless.

Their dance of seduction was as intoxicating as the finest champagne, though there was nothing alcoholic on the menu tonight. The dinner was an agonizing eternity of increasing desire, and P.J. felt a thrill of anticipation race through her when it was finally over.

Connor moved the table aside and drew her to her feet. Gazing down where the taut buds of her nipples thrust forward, begging for his attention, he said, "That's a dangerous dress you're wearin', lass."

"I like living dangerously," P.J. said, mentally consigning her inhibitions to perdition as she boldly wrapped her arms around his neck. He gazed at her with longing in his eyes, and she trembled with her need to be loved by this man. She lifted her lips to his, wanting, needing him.

He groaned and folded her in his arms, burying his hands in her long hair. Slowly, he bent to kiss her. He was so large, yet his kiss so exquisitely gentle, it thrilled P.J. to her toes.

Every nerve ending came achingly alive, anticipating his touch. Eagerly she pressed herself against him and put her heart and soul into the kiss. Connor groaned and tightened his hold, molding her against his body until P.J. felt herself warmed clear through by his heat—and intensely aware of the rigid evidence of his desire. His eyes darkened and he slanted his mouth across hers, holding back nothing.

He stole her breath away with that devastating kiss, filled with passion, desire and a deep-seated need. As she drew back to clear her senses, his hooded gaze raked her body. Gone was the amiable Irishman she'd come to know and love. In his place was a primitive male whose control was being sorely tested.

A thrill shot through her and she arched against him in instinctive response. His large hand cupped her bottom, as he claimed her mouth even more fiercely than before. Kneading the sensitive flesh of her buttocks, he created a warm flood of moisture deep within her.

Skin—she had to feel his skin against hers. She slid his jacket off his shoulders, then fumbled with his tie until Connor yanked it off in frustration. Quickly then, she unbuttoned his crisp white shirt, and with one swift movement Connor pulled it off and discarded it. P.J. let her fingers roam through the sprinkling of red-gold hairs on his chest, glorying in the crisp feel of them.

Her breasts were so tight now, they positively ached. She pressed them against the solid bulwark of his chest, hoping for some measure of relief.

Connor tipped her head up and gazed at her with a questioning look in his eyes as he responded to her need and slowly palmed one of her breasts through her dress. Her eyes closed involuntarily as he stroked the hardened peak with his thumb. "Yes," she breathed.

"Open your eyes, lass," he said softly. "Look at me."

She opened her eyes and gazed into his. The primitive male stared back, his face cast into shadows by the flickering candlelight. "You must be sure, lass," he said, his voice husky with primal need. "If I go any further, I won't be able to stop."

She'd never been more sure of anything in her life. She nodded and slid the dress off her shoulders, letting it pool in a cloud of rose pink at her feet.

He gazed at her with hungry eyes. "My God, you're beautiful," he said in hushed, reverent tones. "But there's one thing I'll be needin' to tell you—"

"Not now," P.J. said, and pressed herself against him, skin to skin. Connor groaned, then swept her into his arms and deposited her gently on the bed, smoothing the dark hair out of her eyes. As he hungrily took one aching breast into his mouth, she surrendered to the passion wrought by his loving hands and mouth.

He divested her of her panties, and impatiently she fumbled with his belt until he yanked off the rest of his clothes and stood before her in naked splendor.

She inhaled sharply. Dear Lord, the man was gorgeous. He stood proudly, enduring her scrutiny as she ran her gaze down the length of his body. His strong, muscled chest tapered to a flat stomach and narrow waist. Below, his sex jutted out at the juncture of powerful thighs. Her eyes widened and her gaze turned back to his face, seeing the fierce animal pleasure kindle in his eyes as he let her look her fill.

She rose and reached out for him, knowing only that she had to touch him—now. She stroked the length of his beautifully muscled body and grasped his rigid maleness in her hand. He threw his head back and groaned in pleasure. Loving the feeling of power it gave her, P.J. continued to caress him until his breathing came in ragged gasps and his powerful hands pulled her away.

Swiftly he dragged her down to the bed and renewed the play of his hands and mouth on the secret places of her body until he had her moaning and writhing in desire. He didn't let her linger there, but brought her to the edge of passion and beyond. Only when she was fully satisfied did he sheathe himself to protect her.

He entered her then, filling her completely with a sense of absolute rightness. His strong, sure thrusts built an agonizing tension in her as he gently but firmly cradled her beneath his body. The pleasure rose in waves about her until his pace quickened and she convulsed in one glorious release. He joined her, their primitive cries a testimony to the unbridled passion they shared.

P.J. sighed. Now that . . . that was magic.

She came out of her daze to find Connor still arched above her, his face the embodiment of fulfilled desire. He looked down at her, the primitive male gone. Her mischievous leprechaun was back. "That . . . that was . . ."

"Was what? Magic?" she teased.

He relaxed and eased down beside her, holding her close, still joined in the most intimate way. "I...I can't think of a word grand enough to describe that experience." He gave her an affectionate look and smoothed the hair off her brow. "You're a rare delight, lass. I never dreamed it would...could be... like this."

She shivered as the cold air touched her body and he gathered her close to warm her. He looked around, apparently coming to the belated realization they were still on top of the bed covers. "Let's get you warm, shall we?"

"Don't go," she muttered sleepily as he pulled her to her feet.

He pulled the sheet back, them bundled her into the bed and lay down beside her, sheltering them both with the covers. "Don't worry, lass, I'm not going anywhere."

Drowsy, she snuggled up close to him, feeling this had to be one of the best moments of her life.

"Lass, there's just one thing I have to ask."

"Mmm-hmm?"

"What's your true name?" he whispered.

She chuckled sleepily and yawned. "Oh, no, you don't. You're not getting it out of me that easily."

Even as sleepy as she was, she felt him stiffen. "Whas wrong?" she slurred.

"Nothing, lass," he muttered. "Nothing at all. Just go to sleep."

P.J. smiled against his shoulder as she let herself fall asleep, glad she'd let her inhibitions go and made love with Connor. He was worth it.

CONNOR WOKE in gradual stages, eventually becoming aware that he lay in bed spoon fashion with a very warm—and very naked—P.J. The events of the night before came flooding back in a rush as the feel of P.J.'s bottom nestled against his groin prompted him to firm in response.

He groaned to himself. He wanted nothing more than to snug up against the cleft of her buttocks, to feel her turn soft and pliant, warm and passionate, in his arms once more, but it was out of the question.

Slowly, gently, he eased himself out of bed and headed toward the bathroom, closing the door softly so he wouldn't wake her. He splashed cold water on his face and stared blearily into the mirror. The evidence of his desire was reflected there, standing out in brazen splendor.

He glared down at the recalcitrant thing. This small bit of flesh—well, maybe not *that* small—had taken over his body last night and had its way with him, and with P.J.

Oh, Lord. His intentions had been so good, but he hadn't been able to resist P.J.'s artless temptation, or the demands of this piece of flesh. It rose proudly, mocking him even more. "What have you gotten us into?" he muttered at it.

That was a mistake. The memory of exactly what it had gotten into the night before overwhelmed him. P.J. had felt so warm and moist and tight...

"Argh!" He cut the memory off abruptly and stepped into the shower, turning on the cold water full blast. He shivered in the freezing spray, but smiled in grim satisfaction as he glanced down and saw the object of his ire shrivel up and turn blue. "Serves you right," he muttered.

He turned the other spigot to mix the water to body temperature and began soaping up. P.J. was too fine a woman to be treated like a one-night stand, and he respected her too much to take her as a lover when he knew it could never go anywhere. He berated himself for not telling her that the night before, but her ardent response and her simple trust had been his undoing.

Trust—there was that word again. Sure, she'd trusted him enough with the most intimate secrets of her body, but not enough to tell him her real name. Why? Did she know Connor couldn't work any magic on her unless he knew her true name? True, glamarye would work on anyone who didn't have true sight. But to do the really binding, lasting magic, he had to know the person's true name.

Aye, he could ferret it out right enough, by using magic or good old-fashioned mortal detective work, but that wasn't the point. It wasn't that he wanted to know her name so badly. It's just that he wanted to know everything he could about her—and he wanted her to trust him enough to tell him herself.

Connor stepped out of the shower and toweled off. Of course, she'd been half-asleep last night when he'd asked her. Maybe if he tried again this morning . . .

He glanced down, relieved to see he was in full control of his body once again. "Behave yourself," he admonished, and wrapped a towel around his waist, covering his manhood so it wouldn't get any ideas. This time Connor intended to be in full control of *all* parts of his body.

He walked back into the bedroom to see P.J. awake and sitting up, the bedclothes thankfully concealing the glory of her nudity.

She must have seen the guarded look in his eyes, because her smile turned tremulous and tentative. "Good morning." It was more of a question than a statement.

Her simple words brought out Connor's latent protective instincts. Though he was determined to ensure this never happened again, he couldn't destroy her ego, either. She looked so fragile and pale—so vulnerable—he had to reassure her.

He crossed the room and sat down next to her on the bed. Kissing her gently, he said, "And a good mornin' to you, too, lass."

She relaxed visibly and he fingered a lock of her silky black hair. "You bewitched me last night, P.J. P.J....'tis such a harsh name for such a delicate flower as yourself. Tell me, what does the *P* stand for? Paula? Persephone? Or maybe Pollyanna?" He felt like a heel for asking, but he had to know.

She smiled hesitantly. "I told you—it's embarrassing and I'd rather not say."

"I see," he said softly. She still didn't trust him. Sadly, he kissed her softly on the forehead. "Well, we've a suspect to interview in a couple of hours, so we'd best be getting ready, don't you think?"

P.J. gave him a puzzled look but nodded and departed for her own room. Connor followed his own advice and dressed, trying to come to terms with the feelings roiling inside him. Why was learning her name so important to him—and what was the matter with him lately, anyway? He didn't seem to be able to control his body or his mind anymore.

P.J. Sheridan—she was the reason. Aye, the lass had his emotions so mixed up he could swear she was a nymph or a sprite—or one of the original faeries who had played such havoc with mortal hormones in times past. Unfortunately he knew she was none of those things. If she were, he wouldn't have to worry about courting her.

Court her? Where had that thought come from? He stopped abruptly in his dressing, stunned by the implications. Yes, he wanted to court her, to explore this developing relationship of theirs and see how far it would take them. With her whimsical sense of humor, her loving attitude and deep abiding wish to believe in magic, Connor knew P.J. was a woman he could love, maybe even marry.

He sighed and jerked his pants on with unnecessary force. But, saints preserve us, he'd sworn to marry only one of the Fae. How could he have known he'd meet and fall for a mortal? He'd have to nip this in the bud now, before it went too far. And what's worse, he had to tell P.J. why.

P.J. HEARD A KNOCK on the adjoining door and opened it to see Connor standing there, looking sexy as hell in his casual photographer's gear. "You're early...." Her voice trailed off as she noted the set look on Connor's face.

Her heart sinking, she asked, "What's wrong?" What *could* be wrong after the wonderful night they'd shared together?

"I have to tell you something."

"What?"

Connor raked a hand through his hair. "Last night should never have happened—I shouldn't have made love to you, lass. It wasn't right."

A sharp pain lanced through her, followed by a feeling of dread. She had a feeling she wasn't going to like this. "Why...why not?"

He turned to look at her, his expression reflecting the pain and agony she felt. "I can't take advantage of you. You're too good, too fine—and I've promised my people I'll not commit myself to any lass but one of the Fae, preferably one with magic as strong as my own."

P.J.'s heart almost rent in two. That damned delusion of his again! "That's ridic—"

"Nay, lass, it wouldn't be fair to you."

Confused, and starting to get a little angry, P.J. said, "Let me get this straight. You're saying that you can't marry me, right?"

Connor nodded, his expression glum.

"Well, who asked you to?" Irritated at the surprised look on Connor's face, P.J. fumed anew. Okay, so she'd been daydreaming along those lines, but it had only been wishful thinking. With his belief in the little people, she knew it would never work. "How arrogant can you get? One night of making love and you assume I want to be shackled to you for life?"

Connor spread his hands in bewilderment. "I didn't mean—"

"And if you're so all-fired worried about my feelings, why'd you wait until *now* to tell me? Why didn't you tell me this last night?"

"I tried to tell you but...I lost my head, lass. I meant for last night to be merely a romantic dinner for two. I didn't mean to get carried away, but you were so soft and warm and sweet, you were irresistible." His expression was sad, pleading for understanding.

Her insides quivered anew at the memory of exactly how good they'd been together. "Yeah, you were pretty irresistible yourself," P.J. muttered.

Hope kindled in Connor's eyes, but she hardened her heart to him. "But since I don't have faerie blood, and I'm not good enough for you—"

"'Tisn't that, lass—"

She swept over his protestations. "Then let's just forget it ever happened, okay?"

Her anger must have shown in her eyes, for Connor said, "Will you be wanting to call the whole thing off, then? Forget the rest of the interviews?"

She pondered that briefly but discarded it. She wasn't giving up on him that easily. "No. No, I'll stick by our agreement. But let's try to keep it professional, shall we?"

Yes, professional. Until he could admit his delusions were just that she wasn't about to let him make love to her again, no matter how much she wanted to. She just hoped it wouldn't take too long. Damn it, she wasn't going to let his unfounded beliefs and overdeveloped sense of responsibility keep them apart.

Faerie king, my great-aunt Martha's behind!

Connor nodded sadly. "All right, lass. We'll do it your way. And thanks."

P.J. nodded briskly and grabbed her briefcase, then said in her best no-nonsense tone, "Okay, let's go. Our next suspect, Madame Cherelle, is meeting us for breakfast at a café in Montmartre."

Chapter Seven

As they took the metro to Montmartre, P.J. was grateful Connor did as she asked and kept the conversation strictly business. Though it pained her to see Connor so cool and aloof when yesterday had been so wonderful, P.J. ignored the pain in her heart and reminded herself it was for the best.

"How familiar are you with Madame Cherelle's work?" he asked.

"I know her as a debunker of false mystics, but she's best known as a psychic. A psychic who debunks other psychics is so unusual, I've been wanting to meet her. I figure she must either be a very gifted charlatan herself, to be able to spot others, or—"

"Or she's truly psychic," Connor said.

P.J. cast him a sideways glance as they exited the metro. "Well, I guess we know what your opinion is."

"Aye, but not for the reason you're thinkin'. Remember I told you Stayle had identified Madame Cherelle as a member of the Fae?"

"Oh, yes, that's right." She kept forgetting how consistent his delusions were.

"Well, that's why I'm fairly certain her abilities are real. Stayle tells me she has quite a bit of pixie in her—that's what gives her the sight."

So this woman had faerie blood? Terrific. That's just what P.J. needed—for Connor to meet a woman he believed was one of the Fae—a woman he *could* marry.

P.J. shot him a suspicious glance. Could that be one of the reasons he'd been so eager to make this trip? To meet a sexy French pixie? Viciously P.J. hoped the woman was married with six screaming kids.

They found the café, and since they were early they ordered hot chocolate and croissants. When their order came Connor asked after Madame Cherelle in what sounded like excellent French. The proprietor shrugged and gestured expressively toward the door.

They turned in that direction to see a tiny elderly woman enter, leaning on a cane for support. Small-boned and delicate, she looked exactly like the pixie Connor claimed she was.

The first thing P.J. felt was relief. The woman might not have six screaming kids at home, but Connor couldn't possibly see her as a matrimonial prospect.

The relief faded, replaced by disbelief. This was the famous psychic debunker? She looked more like someone's sweet white-haired grandmother, not like the woman known for her ruthlessness in exposing charlatans.

Connor rose and took the woman's hand to escort her to their table. Obviously accustomed to chivalry, Madame Cherelle allowed Connor to cater to her, seemingly oblivious of the strange picture they made together as he hulked over her, at least three times her size.

P.J. suppressed a smile. Connor was naturally solicitous, which was a good cover for him to press his talisman ring against the woman's hand. He gave P.J. a faint shake of the head, indicating that he had cleared Madame of any wrongdoing. P.J. sighed in relief—for some reason, she didn't want this woman to be the thief.

Madame Cherelle seated herself next to P.J. and gave her a sweet smile. "You must be the American writer, yes?" she asked in beautiful English with only a trace of a charming accent.

"Yes, Madame, I'm P. J. Sheridan, and this is my photographer, Connor Michaels."

Connor bobbed his head at her and greeted her in French. They conversed for a few moments in that beautiful, mellifluous language, then she said, "Excuse us, Mademoiselle Sheridan. We did not mean to exclude you, but it is rare to find an American who speaks my language so beautifully."

P.J. couldn't help smiling at this charming, gracious lady. "I understand. Tell me, did you wear the shoes you purchased at Something Extra?"

Madame glanced down at her feet. "*Oui*, mademoiselle, as you requested."

P.J.'s gaze followed Madame's, down to her feet. The shoes were a modest pair of pumps made of handsome brown leather with a wedge-shaped low heel. The topstitching was picked out in a contrasting beige that matched the color of the heel, and the toe was decorated with a series of punched holes in a design P.J. recognized as the yin-yang symbol.

These were fantasy shoes? She'd expected something far more exotic after seeing the others. These looked so...sensible.

Remembering her promise to keep an open mind, P.J. narrowed her eyes and concentrated hard for a moment, trying to see if she could pick up an impression of the woman's personality from the supposed magic in her shoes.

Yes, her initial impression was still strong. Sensible was the operative word here, along with honesty, and a touch of otherworldliness that gave the woman a piquant charm. Is this what Stayle had intended?

Her confusion must have shown on her face, for the elderly woman's face wrinkled into a smile and she chuckled. "You are thinking I paid too much for such a drab pair of shoes, no?"

Not at all taken aback, P.J. laughed. "Well, yes, I was," she admitted. "The others I've seen were rather ornate, gaudy even. Why are yours so plain—and why did you decide to buy a pair, anyway?"

Madame shrugged. "It's not so hard to understand. I journeyed to Denver last month to investigate a new psychic whose powers are said to rival those of Uri Geller. His pretensions were easily unmasked, and since I was so close to Vail and had several days to wait for my flight back, I decided to visit the boutique. I couldn't resist investigating a store that claimed to make magic shoes. You are doing the same, no?"

P.J. nodded. "And what did you find?" Had the famous debunker been taken in?

"I found Stayle O'Flaherty, a truly gifted designer of wonderful shoes. Since I couldn't determine the credibility of her claims without experiencing her magic for myself, I bought a pair."

"But why are yours so plain?"

The woman smiled slightly and patted P.J.'s hand. "I'm an old woman and have no need for fancy shoes. After a lovely chat, Mademoiselle O'Flaherty reviewed my personality profile and recommended these."

Madame held out her foot and twisted her ankle back and forth to get a good look at the shoes. Connor finally seemed to remember what he was there for and began to take pictures.

"Tell me, *ma petite,*" the old woman said. "What impression did the shoes give you?"

As P.J. hesitated, Madame Cherelle shook her head in admonition. "Don't try to be polite. Be honest and tell me what you saw."

P.J. considered for a moment. "Sensible. That's what I first thought when I saw them—that you were sensible."

P.J. could see Connor grinning behind his camera, and the elderly woman gifted her with a smile, as if P.J. were her star pupil. "*Très bien!* That was *exactement* the image we were trying to project."

"Sensibility? But why?"

"When you're a psychic—especially one who goes around exposing charlatans—it is very important to ensure your potential client trusts you. Psychics have a bad reputation and I needed something to counteract my clients' fears."

"So you'd say the shoes work for you?"

The woman nodded. "*Absolument.*"

"But what about their claims?" P.J. persisted. "Do you believe these shoes are magic?"

"*Oui.* I'm certain they do possess the magic that is claimed for them."

This from one of the most famous debunkers of their age? P.J. stared speculatively at her. "How can you be so sure?"

"I can't tell you that," the woman said serenely.

Connor stopped taking pictures and leaned down to whisper something in the woman's ear.

She patted his cheek. "I thought your resemblance to Mademoiselle O'Flaherty had to be more than just coincidence." Turning back to P.J., she said, "I know they have magic, because his sister has magic—she proved it when her talisman turned my aura to gold."

P.J. hoped she didn't look as startled as she felt. "Gold?" she managed to croak out.

"Aye, gold," said Connor. "I told you Madame Cherelle was part faerie—that's how the talisman identified her."

"I see," P.J. responded, not at all sure she did. How had Connor persuaded this woman to corroborate his story? Was his charm such that he had only to whisper in her ear and she'd make up any lie to support him? No, P.J. decided reluctantly, Connor wasn't *that* good, and besides, Madame's sterling reputation belied that.

"*Oui,*" Madame said. "And it explains why the vision is so strong in me."

P.J. was totally baffled. The Frenchwoman had an unimpeachable reputation for debunking charlatans, but as far as P.J. knew, she'd never been investigated herself. Reluctant to display her rude skepticism before this gracious lady, P.J. merely glanced obliquely at her.

Madame laughed. "You do not believe me, I can tell. Shall I convince you?"

P.J. had to be honest. "You can try." She glanced balefully at Connor to forestall any amused comments. Surprisingly, he seemed subdued, almost reverent as he gazed at the elderly woman.

"Okay, I will show you." The woman took P.J.'s hand in hers.

Warily, P.J. said, "What are you going to do?" Familiar with the wailing and theatrics of charlatans, P.J. was reluctant to be involved in that kind of scene in such a public place.

"I'm just going to hold your hand. You see my ring?"

P.J. nodded. The large oval-cut amethyst was hard to miss.

Madame turned it so the stone faced under her hand toward the palm. "This is my talisman—the amethyst enhances my natural abilities. I always knew the stone helped me, but until I met Mademoiselle O'Flaherty, I didn't know why." Madame gently clasped P.J.'s hand so the amethyst fit squarely in the center of P.J.'s palm and closed her eyes.

As P.J. watched her in trepidation, she felt the stone grow warm in her hand—a pleasant kind of warmth, not at all uncomfortable. Thank heavens, Madame's face remained serene and she didn't start flinging her limbs about or start making dreadful gurgling noises like some so-called psychics did. In fact, the only movement P.J. could discern was the faint twitching of Madame's eyelids.

After a couple of minutes Madame Cherelle sighed and opened her eyes, releasing P.J.'s hand. *"C'est ça,"* she said. "That wasn't so bad, was it, *ma petite?"*

P.J. shook her head, trying to decide if she was disappointed that Madame hadn't acted like all the others, or relieved. A moment of doubt assailed her. Could it be the Frenchwoman was so different because she really was psychic?

Connor leaned forward, an intent look on his face. "What did you see?"

Madame frowned a little and turned to P.J. "Your future is strangely clouded, difficult to see, as if there were something or someone interfering with my vision. I saw you in the mountains, in danger—"

"Danger?" Connor interrupted. "What kind of danger?"

"A...a man. A bad man—a thief. She is in danger from him." Madame turned urgently back to P.J. "Though perilous, this will be the most important moment of your life. From it, you may conquer your malady and achieve the greatest joy of your existence—if you make the correct decision." Madame grasped her hand again. "Do you understand? You must make the correct decision!"

"Yes, I understand," P.J. said, not knowing what else to say. She was baffled. The psychic had sounded so authentic at first, what with her revelation about the thief, but P.J. didn't have any malady that she knew of. And what was her greatest joy?

P.J. opened her mouth to ask more questions, then closed it. She didn't have the right to question Madame Cherelle as if she were a phony. P.J. wasn't investigating her, and she owed it to this gracious woman, so unlike the charlatans she'd met and unmasked, to act as if she believed Madame was telling the truth. Grilling her would just be bad manners.

P.J. smiled reassuringly at Connor, and he sighed almost imperceptibly. "Are you all right?" he asked Madame.

The old woman raised a shaky hand to her forehead. "Forgive me. I'm not as young as I once was, and this drains me. If you'll excuse me, I need to be alone to gather my senses—some *café* wouldn't come amiss, either."

Connor nodded and ordered her a cup of coffee. They said their goodbyes and boarded the metro back toward the hotel. "What did you whisper in her ear?" P.J. asked.

"Only that I was Stayle's brother and we knew she was faerie."

"Nothing else? Nothing about the theft of the shoehorn?"

"Nay, lass, 'twasn't necessary."

P.J. nodded abstractedly. He really hadn't had time to do that. "Then I wonder how she knew."

"Knew what?"

"Knew that we were looking for a thief."

Connor just raised an eyebrow and flashed his dimple at her. "I'm thinking you'll not be liking the answer."

"Magic, I suppose," she said mildly. P.J. couldn't even summon up enough indignation to respond as he obviously expected her to.

"Aye," Connor said with a surprised look on his face. "Do you mean you'll be after believing me now?"

P.J. shook her head. No, she still didn't believe Connor was a leprechaun. But maybe, just maybe, Madame was a real psychic. Excitement rose within her. If so, then maybe magic was real after all!

CONNOR'S HOPES ROSE. P.J. had actually sounded as if she was weakening, that she might have finally started believing in magic.

As they entered their hotel he repeated his question. "Do you believe me now?"

"I—I'm not sure...." The puzzled look on her face turned to annoyance as her eyes narrowed on something behind him. "Oh, no. Not again!" She grabbed his sleeve. "Don't turn around. Maybe he won't see us."

Connor did as she asked. "Who is it?"

P.J. sighed. "Never mind. It's too late."

"Well, hello!" said a voice from behind him. Connor's patience almost vanished. He knew that voice.

Slowly he turned and confirmed his suspicions. Neil Chalmers, damn him. Why did the man always have to turn up like a bad shilling where he wasn't wanted? First New York, now Paris.

Neil waved a rolled-up newspaper at them. "Wow, isn't this a coincidence? It must be fate. You do believe in fate, don't you?" Neil babbled as he approached.

"No," P.J. said in a clipped tone.

"So," Neil said cheerily, bouncing on the balls of his feet as he tapped the newspaper in his palm.

"Destiny has brought us together again. You ought to listen, P.J.—fate is telling you to heed my offer. You were *born* to be my elf queen."

Connor snorted in disgust as P.J. grimaced. "I told you," she said, enunciating every word very carefully, "I'm not interested in acting."

"Yes," Connor said in exasperation. "Can't you take a hint?"

Neil breezily waved it away. "Nonsense. Everyone wants to be in the movies. Besides, I have information you need."

Connor raised a disbelieving eyebrow. "And what will that be?"

"Oh, just a little something on that shoe store P.J. is investigating—a juicy little tidbit that will help her prove there's no magic in the shoes."

"Oh?" said P.J., sounding interested. "Like what?"

"Well," Neil said in a confiding manner, "it seems Stayle O'Flaherty's brother was some kind of bigwig in stocks or something. He quit under very suspicious circumstances and poured all his money into his sister's store. How much would you like to bet he made this whole magic thing up just to make sure his sister's little shop would be a success?"

What a disgusting troll. Connor clenched his fists, sorry that he laid claim to being a gentleman, even sorrier that Neil was so much smaller than him. It wouldn't even be a fair fight.

"Sorry, Chalmers, but that's old news," P.J. informed him. "And it doesn't prove anything."

"You mean the shoes really do have magic?" Neil's eyes widened. "How does it work?"

"I meant no such thing," P.J. said. "I'm sorry, but we must be going. I . . . I'm expecting an important phone call."

Connor grinned. P.J. was a lousy liar, but Neil certainly couldn't call her bluff without looking like a cretin himself.

P.J. brushed by Neil, who backpedaled hastily, taking himself out of Connor's reach as Connor followed P.J. across the hotel lobby to the concierge.

"Have there been any calls for me?" she asked in a penetrating voice.

Neil had started to follow them, but upon receiving a glare from Connor, he changed his mind and scurried away.

The concierge checked P.J.'s box. "No, mademoiselle, there are no telephone calls for you."

"Thank you. Is he gone?" she muttered out of the side of her mouth.

"No. He's still lurking near the elevators, trying to appear as if he's not looking at us." Connor fingered a silky strand of P.J.'s hair. "Who would've thought P.J. Sheridan—the honest, upright citizen—would've stooped to lyin'? I'm that shocked at you, lass," he said with a grin.

P.J. glared at him and turned to the concierge. "May I use your phone?"

The concierge nodded and moved away to serve another customer. P.J. picked up the receiver and pretended to talk into it. "You don't fool me, Mr. O'Flaherty. You'd be just as glad to get rid of Neil as I would." She paused, a pensive look on her face. "Don't you find it odd that he's shown up twice now? That's a bit too much for coincidence."

"Aye, lass, that it is. What is it you're thinking?"

Her brow creased in a frown. "I just remembered—when you and Melissa were playing footsie out on the porch—"

"Footsie?" he repeated incredulously.

"Yes, footsie. Anyway, when I went inside to get her drink, Neil was sitting next to my briefcase. Then later, when I gave you a copy of the itinerary, there was one missing. I'll bet—"

"The sneak took it."

P.J. nodded. "My thoughts exactly. But why would he do such a thing?"

The woman was far too modest. "'Tis obvious. He wants to get to know you better. Whether 'tis for his film or for himself, I'm not certain, but that's what he wants." Whatever Neil's reason, Connor didn't like the idea at all.

P.J. grimaced. "Wonderful. How can we get rid of him?"

"Ah, that's the easy part. We'll just change the itinerary. We'll have to interview the same people, of course, but we'll stay in different hotels so he won't be able to find us."

P.J. nodded. "Good idea. Let's arrange it."

Connor glanced at the elevators. "He's gone now. You can hang up the phone . . . Penelope?"

P.J. just glared at him. He tried again. "No? How about Polygon or maybe Paragon?"

"Look—" P.J. began, only to be interrupted by a voice from across the room.

"Wait! Connor, I must speak with you!" Bernard, the frantic hotel manager, came hurrying across the room.

Bernard was a typical hob. Small, with brown skin and brown hair, he had a face that only a mother—or another hob—could love. Dressed in an impeccably tailored suit that spoke of his British origin, Bernard appeared flustered.

Connor turned to face him, maintaining a polite expression. This was one of his subjects, and his duty dictated courtesy. "Bernard, it's good to see you. I'd like you to meet P. J. Sheridan. P.J., this is our host and my... cousin."

P.J.'s incredulous look took in the disparity in their appearances. "Your cousin?"

"In a matter of speaking, yes." He lowered his voice. "He's one of the Fae—one of my subjects."

P.J. raised one of her eyebrows but declined to comment.

Bernard mopped his brow with a handkerchief. "I didn't know she was... one of us."

Connor shrugged. "She's not, but it's all right. She's helping us find Stayle's stolen talisman."

"I see," said the little man, but he still cast a wary glance at P.J. "Sire, I need to speak to you about a matter of the utmost importance."

"Sire?" P.J. echoed.

Connor grimaced. "I told you not to call me that—not even in private. It's just Connor. And don't worry, you can talk in front of her."

"Perhaps, but I don't really want to discuss this matter in the lobby. Would you mind coming to my office?"

"Certainly," he said. P.J. didn't have any objections, either. In fact, she looked downright eager and *very* curious.

They followed Bernard to his office and, seating himself next to the desk, Connor said, "Now, what is it you're needing?"

Bernard shuddered. "It's horrible. Just horrible. One of our security guards was a little careless this morning.... He lost his weapon!"

"Lost it? What do you mean?" When Bernard appeared too agitated to speak, Connor said soothingly, "Just calm down and tell me everything that happened."

Bernard took a few deep breaths and tried again. "It was early this morning, around two a.m. He left his station for a few moments to, er, use the facilities, and left his pistol in the desk at his station. It wasn't loaded, of course, but when he came back it was gone!"

"I see. And what is it you'll be wanting me to do?"

"Who knows what nefarious purposes the perpetrator might have in mind? I can't expose my guests to a murdering psychopath," the little man wailed.

"Now, don't fash yourself, Bernard. What d'you want me to do?"

"Could you...could you use your magic to find the firearm and the person who took it?"

"Aye," Connor agreed, grinning. "That I could."

Finally, this was his chance to use real magic and show P.J. he was telling the truth. After all, it was his duty as king of the Fae to use it to assist his subjects whenever they requested—so long as the request was reasonable. And this request was more than reasonable. He'd be able to kill two birds with one stone.

P.J. cast him a doubtful look and Connor grinned at her.

"It may be a bit difficult, though, since the gun probably has more than a wee bit o' iron in it. Iron," he reminded them, "interferes with a spell something awful."

P.J.'s look seemed to say she knew he'd find some way to weasel out if the magic didn't work.

Bernard shuddered. "I know...but could you try?"

"Why can't you just do it yourself?" P.J. asked Bernard.

Bernard gave her a horrified look. "I'm a hob, not a leprechaun."

Connor took pity on her and explained. "Hob magic is more suited to keeping the home and hearth, and is limited to that, whilst a leprechaun's magic is basically boundless, though not without price, of course."

"Oh. Of course," P.J. said, looking thoroughly unconvinced.

"Now, Bernard, do you have anything the gun was touching, perchance?"

"Yes. Yes, of course. I have the holster." Bernard reached into his desk drawer and pulled out the brown leather holster. Touching it with only his thumb and forefinger, he dropped it on the desk with a look of distaste.

Connor picked it up and held it in his hands, trying to get some sense of the weapon that had rested there recently. Closing his eyes, he focused on the power in his talisman ring and drew on the strength of his magic. Bit by bit, he constructed the incantation in his mind, a simple spell that would show him the identity of the people who had touched the holster in the past twenty-four hours.

The spell built, he quickly muttered the appropriate Gaelic words and focused his power *through* the ring to touch the core of his magic.

Slowly the images coalesced in his mind. They appeared in reverse order, working backward from the present.

Connor, reaching out to accept the holster from Bernard as P.J. looked on.

An agitated uniformed guard handing the holster to Bernard.

The guard staring at the empty holster with a horrified look on his face.

Then, finally, the scene he'd been waiting for:

The gun sitting in its holster in the desk. An indistinct figure reaching for it—

Suddenly everything went gray and fuzzy. With a curse, Connor cut the vision off.

He opened his eyes to find Bernard and P.J. staring at him: one in anxiety and the other in suspicion. Connor grimaced. Terrific. Why did his magic have to fail him now, just when he needed it most?

"Well?" Bernard demanded impatiently. "Did you learn who purloined it?"

Connor shook his head sadly. "No, I'm sorry, Bernard. I tried to get a look at the thief, but there was something interfering."

P.J. raised a disbelieving eyebrow. "The iron, I suppose?"

"No, no... it was more as if the thief used a masking spell, or something was disrupting my ability to sense him magically."

"You mean the perpetrator is... one of us?" Bernard asked in horror.

"It certainly looks that way," Connor admitted. "Do you know of anyone locally who would misuse their power in such a way?"

"No," Bernard said. "Not really. There are some bad apples hereabouts, but they know better than to come into my hotel, and I have wards out to watch for them. If one of them had entered, I would have known it."

"You mean there are good faeries and bad faeries?" P.J. obviously had trouble suppressing a grin.

Bernard's answering look was full of disgust. "Of course. Just as there are good mortals and bad mortals."

Connor couldn't resist a chance to tease her. "Yes, after all, we're only...faerie."

P.J. just grimaced at the bad joke. Ignoring the by-play, Bernard said, "But surely you could try a different spell, one to show us where the pistol is at this moment."

"I could," Connor said, "but I doubt it would do much good if it's in the possession of this bad faerie."

P.J. chuckled and Bernard cast her a dirty look.

"I'm sorry," she said around a grin, "but if you knew how silly that sounds..."

Bernard merely huffed and turned his back on her. "It is no laughing matter, I assure you. Sire, please, perform the spell."

Connor obliged him and focused his power once more, this time to get a mental image of the gun's surroundings. Slowly the image took shape. The gun appeared to be wrapped in some sort of cloth and hidden in a dark drawer somewhere. The thief wasn't touching it, so the image was quite clear, but it was so dark he could glean few details.

He gave up, terminating the spell, and told them what he'd seen. "I'm sorry I can't do any better," he said with real regret. His people so seldom asked anything of him that it bothered him when he couldn't satisfy this simple request.

Bernard wrung his hands. "Isn't there anything else you can do?"

Connor shook his head. "No, I'm afraid not. I can't even locate it properly—the iron in the gun throws off the results." An idea came to him. "But we might be able to determine how it will be used in the near future. What do you fear the most?"

"Well, of course, I hope it is never used against another human being, mortal or faerie, but I am most worried that it will be used against one of my guests. Why?"

"No problem, then. Go see Madame Cherelle—she's one of us, a pixie soothsayer. She should be able to tell you if and when something of the sort will happen."

Bernard frowned, obviously unhappy.

"It's all right, Bernard. You can charge it to me."

Bernard nodded and thanked him profusely. It just made Connor feel guiltier. He hadn't actually done anything, after all. Everything he'd tried had backfired on him, but Madame Cherelle might have better luck.

He escorted P.J. to their rooms. "What would you think, lass, about changing our plans? Instead of leaving tomorrow mornin', what d'you say we leave tonight and find a different hotel to stay in so we can avoid the pesky Neil? After all, 'tis Ireland we're going to, and I've many more relatives to choose from.''

P.J. agreed instantly. "Great. The sooner this is over, the better."

Connor frowned. Her meaning was plain. She couldn't wait for this to be over—and to get away from him. For a fleeting moment he wished he knew her true name so he could cast a spell to make her forget all that had happened and they could start all over again.

Guilt assailed him and he sighed heavily. No, it wouldn't be fair to her. The evening flight was a better idea. It would keep him from succumbing to his baser instincts with the irresistible—and wholly mortal—Miss Sheridan.

But... if she decided she didn't care for the consequences and tried to seduce *him,* well, he wouldn't be responsible for the outcome. A leprechaun could only take so much.

Chapter Eight

Connor shifted the rental car into gear as he and P.J. traveled to interview the fourth suspect, a shipping tycoon named Patrick Shaughnessy. It might be irrational, but he felt much better now that he was back on Irish soil. It buoyed his spirits, making him more confident they would eventually find their thief.

Unfortunately it hadn't changed his feelings for P.J., nor hers for him. Even now she edged away from him, trying to put as much distance between them as possible. But every time he shifted gears in the small space, his hand grazed her leg or her arm, making the attraction between them sizzle and spark until the air fairly pulsated with it.

He rolled the window down, trying to get some fresh air—anything to clear this charged atmosphere. Regardless of what had—or, rather, what *hadn't*—happened last night, there was no denying the strong attraction between them. If they didn't come to grips with it pretty soon, it might well do them in.

P.J.'s voice woke him from his reverie.

"I'm sorry, lass," he said. "I was doing a bit of woolgatherin'. What did you say?"

She cleared her throat again, obviously trying to make conversation to break the tension. "Oh, nothing, I just said I'm tired of traveling. There are only two suspects left—I sure hope this guy is the one."

"Bite your tongue!"

P.J. looked definitely taken aback. "What?"

"You'll not be hoping an Irishman is the thief, will you?"

"Well, no, I—"

"I'm seein' this man only as a courtesy to you, so that you can get additional information for your article. I doubt he's the one."

"For heaven's sake, you don't know the man is innocent. Why, you admitted there were good and bad faeries . . . so why can't there be good and bad Irishmen?"

"Well, 'tis possible, I suppose. But the man is filthy rich. What would be the point?"

"So are most of the other suspects. Yet I don't see you using the same arguments for them." She cast him a concerned glance. "It seems you're protesting just a bit too much."

Connor scowled in frustration. He didn't want to admit it, but he, too, suspected the shipping tycoon might be the thief. If Connor's bad luck continued, it was sure to be the one person he didn't want it to be. "Mayhap you're right," he muttered. "But I pray you're wrong."

P.J. patted his hand. Connor was sure she meant it to be reassuring, but it had just the opposite effect. The simple gesture caused a bolt of desire to streak through him like a single-minded spell headed straight for his libido.

Why, if he didn't know better, he'd swear P.J. was part nymph for the spell she was casting on him. His hands clenched on the steering wheel as he restrained himself from returning the gesture, with interest. This mortal was not for him.

Thank heavens, they reached Shaughnessy's country manor then. Connor exhaled an explosive sigh of relief and exited the confines of the car as quickly as he could—out of range of her beguiling presence.

P.J. shot out just as quickly, and they both hurried to the door, avoiding each other's eyes. He knocked, and a maidservant escorted them into the den, where a burly silver-haired gentleman sat waiting for them in a cozy, intimate grouping around the welcome heat of a fireplace.

Shaughnessy looked like a cagy old codger with the map of Ireland on his face—not at all what Connor had expected. The man looked more as if he belonged on the docks than officiating in a boardroom.

Connor strode forward, hand outstretched, eager to touch the man's palm and ascertain, once and for all, if he was the thief.

Shaughnessy rose and held up his bandaged right hand apologetically. "I'm sorry I cannot greet ye properly," he said. "A small accident at the office yesterday. Please, won't ye have a seat?" He gestured toward the other two seats in front of the fireplace.

Connor shared a glance with P.J. This didn't look good. How could he clear the man of any wrongdoing if he couldn't even touch his hand?

They seated themselves and P.J. introduced herself and Connor.

At Connor's polite acknowledgment, Shaughnessy gave him a speculative look. "Is that an Irish brogue I hear? I thought ye were American."

Connor grinned. "Aye, that I am, but my great-grandparents came from County Cork, and I've always considered myself to be Irish. After all, 'if you're lucky enough to be Irish . . .'"

They finished the phrase in unison. "'. . . you're lucky enough.'"

They both chuckled and Connor's resolve to prove Shaughnessy's innocence strengthened. Not only was the man Irish, but Connor liked him.

P.J. poised her pen over the notepad. "Mr. Shaughnessy, as I explained before I'm doing a story on the Something Extra boutique. I understand you bought a pair of shoes there?"

The man nodded toward his feet. "Yes, I did. They don't look like much, do they?"

Connor and P.J. focused their attention on Shaughnessy's feet. He was right—they didn't look like much.

They were plain brown loafers, much like those Connor himself wore, but they carried that distinctive Stayle O'Flaherty difference. The shoes looked brand-new, yet molded to the man's feet like a pair of comfortable old slippers. And, rather than having well-defined seams and topstitching, the lines seemed to blur into each other so that the entire shoe looked as though it had been made from a single piece of leather, created just for that purpose.

"Yes . . . and no," P.J. replied. "They appear plain at first, yet they're somehow altogether . . . extraordinary. Is that what they're supposed to convey of your personality?"

She glanced at Connor and he nodded. Yes, this was the impression Stayle had intended—he could feel the effects of the magic from here. The man might look like a comfortable old shoe, but there was something unique, something special about him. He had to capture that on film. Connor rose to start taking pictures.

The man sighed. "I suppose 'tis, at least that's what my wife says."

P.J. gave him a curious look. "You sound as if you don't believe her. Why did you agree to purchase the shoes, then?"

He shrugged. "She talked me into them. Y'see, she's a bit enamored of anything smacking of mysticism or magic, and when she learned about the magic shoes, there was nothing for it but that I had to have a pair."

"For you, not for herself?"

"Aye, she'll have it that I don't get enough respect and she was certain sure the shoes would do the trick."

"And have they?"

Shaughnessy gave them a wry smile. "Now, I'll not be saying they have, and I'll not be saying they haven't. 'Tis a wee bit early to know yet, but I'll not be doubting that lately I have been treated with a mite more... deference than usual. 'Tisn't me who has the problem, ye understand, but in the social circles me wife likes to run in, 'tis important to her." He shrugged. "It makes her happy."

P.J. smiled at him and Connor could tell she liked the old man as much as he did. "So, Mr. Shaughnessy," P.J. said, "you must be a smart, hardheaded businessman to have come as far as you have. Would you say the shoes have magic?"

The man's face creased in another smile. "I may be a businessman, but I'm Irish, too. Who am I to say whether 'tis magic or no? That's for the likes of you to determine."

P.J. closed her notebook, a sure sign she was about to wind up the interview. It was too soon—Connor hadn't come up with a plan to touch the man's hand yet.

As P.J. made polite noises prior to leaving, Connor formulated his plan swiftly. Pretending to change the film in his camera, he concentrated on casting a small glamarye.

Gripping his ring to help him focus, Connor called upon his power, murmuring the Gaelic words of the spell and releasing it in a spate of power.

As Shaughnessy gestured with his bandaged right hand, Connor created the illusion of him knocking over the pipe stand and one of the pipes falling to the floor.

"Damn my clumsiness," Shaughnessy muttered, and bent over to pick up the illusory pipe.

Relieved that *someone* could still see his illusions, Connor moved swiftly to grasp the pipe before Shaughnessy's fingers passed through the illusion. "Here, let me."

Under cover of picking up the nonexistent pipe, Connor contrived to touch his talisman ring and the back of his hand to Shaughnessy's as their hands brushed the carpet together.

Connor sighed in relief. There was no telltale tingling, nothing to indicate the man had ever held a talisman in his life. Connor couldn't help grinning as Shaughnessy held the pipe stand and Connor pretended to replace the imaginary pipe.

Once Shaughnessy had escorted them out, P.J. said, "Now what was *that* all about?"

"What, lass?"

"That little ceremony you two did with the pipe stand."

"Ceremony?"

"You know—when I was saying goodbye. All of a sudden you both muttered a few words and bowed down to the carpet, rubbed the back of your hands together, then twiddled with the pipe stand."

Connor chuckled. With her true sight, it must have looked a little strange. "Aye, I imagine that's how it looked to you."

She raised an eyebrow. "So what's your version?"

"Well, lass, you'll not be liking the answer."

P.J. sighed. "I suppose not, but I'd like to hear it, anyway."

"Well, y'see, I had to touch the man's hand before we left, and since I couldn't think of any other way to do it, I worked a bit of glamarye."

"Somehow I knew you'd say that," P.J. muttered.

Connor ignored her. "I made it appear as if he'd knocked over his pipe, and when he leaned over to pick it up, I had to beat him to it, since it was just a glamarye. All illusion, no substance, y'see. I couldn't have the man trying to pick up a pipe that wasn't there. And, saints be praised, I touched his hand in the process."

"And...?" P.J. prompted.

"And he isn't the thief—nary a trace of magic anywhere on his hands," Connor concluded triumphantly.

"Right," P.J. said flatly.

Connor sighed in frustration. She still didn't believe him.

"So, that means there's only one suspect left—our magician," she said.

"Right you are. When is our appointment with the Magnificent Ambrose, anyway?" He felt silly just saying the man's title. What sort of man needed a word like "Magnificent" in front of his name to impress people? He had to be their thief.

P.J. consulted their itinerary. "Not until tomorrow afternoon. We fly out first thing tomorrow morning."

"Good, then I have time to show you a bit of the Ireland I know—the Ireland all the Fae know in their heart."

P.J. WAITED IN THE LOBBY for Connor. He'd dropped her off at her room a half hour earlier with the admonition to dress comfortably, so P.J. had donned blue jeans and layered a sweater over a blouse. With sturdy shoes and a heavy coat, she was ready for anything.

The wait left her with nothing to do but think. That business with Connor and Shaughnessy groveling on the floor had certainly been strange. What was all that about? Connor's explanation was hard to buy, but it sure fit the facts.

P.J. replayed the scene in her mind. Shaughnessy and Connor had leaned over in unison to touch the carpet and rub the backs of their hands together, almost as if they were exchanging some bizarre Irish fraternity greeting or something.

Could that be it? Is that what she'd really seen? No, it was too farfetched. She'd never heard of carpet-fondling lodge brothers before. Besides, such a strange greeting would be awfully difficult to keep secret.

Okay, so they weren't lodge brothers, but maybe... maybe they were old friends and had cooked up this whole thing between them to convince P.J. of Connor's magic.

No, that didn't hold up under scrutiny, either. The demonstration *hadn't* convinced her—it wouldn't have convinced anyone. If they'd wanted to trick her into believing in magic, they had the wherewithal and the time to concoct something far more believable. So, why?

She could just hear her sister saying, "When all else fails, and nothing else explains the unexplainable, whatever is left, however unlikely, must be true." If that was so, P.J. would have to accept that it had been glamarye in action. Then that meant...Connor was on the level.

Her heart soared at the thought. If he really was king of the little people, then she could understand his belief that he could marry only one of the Fae. And if he wasn't? Well, then he was just another huckster spinning her a line—albeit a very convincing one—to get her into bed. Unfortunately, that was an all too feasible explanation.

Her logical reporter persona took over, bringing her wayward heart back to earth. Just because she couldn't think of another reason to explain the event didn't mean a logical reason didn't exist—she just hadn't thought of all the possibilities yet.

So which was he? Faerie king . . . or con man? She sighed heavily. She hadn't been able to prove either one—yet. For now she'd give him the benefit of the doubt. After all, even murderers were presumed innocent until proven guilty.

She smiled, relieved. The decision made her feel better, as if a weight had been lifted from her heart.

Just then Connor emerged from the elevator. "I'm sorry to keep you waitin', lass, but I had a bit of business to take care of." He looked her over, appearing to approve of the way she was dressed. "Are you ready?"

She nodded and they headed out to the rental car, to find "the Ireland all the Fae know in their heart."

They headed into the country, away from the hustle and bustle of the city, chatting comfortably of this and that until Connor said, "Ah, here 'tis."

He pulled the car over to the side of the small winding road at the top of a hill. P.J. could see nothing for miles in any direction but the green hills of Ireland and the rich blue sky.

Connor opened the car door and went to look over the edge, and P.J. moved to stand beside him. He stared wistfully out over the panorama spread below them, the wind blowing fiercely through their hair. "'How sweetly lies old Ireland, emerald green beyond the foam, awakening sweet memories, calling the heart back home,'" he murmured.

"What is it? What have we come to see?"

He grinned at her and hugged her close with one arm. She relaxed against him, telling herself it was only normal to want shelter from the biting wind.

"This," he said, gesturing expansively with his free arm. "All this land, as far as the eye can see—'tis ours."

"Ours?"

"'Tis the heritage of the little people."

"But... there's nothing there." Not a person, not a cottage, not even a fence as far as she could see. Only the rolling green hills and natural wild beauty of the land.

He sighed. "Aye, and that's the way 'twill stay. One of my predecessors, a former king of the Fae, began buying land here in Ireland and I've continued the tradition."

"It's yours, then?"

"Nay, lass. 'Tis in the name of the Fae—Faerie Folk, Inc., to be exact. What else?"

What else, indeed? She supposed it had a strange kind of logic. After all, who would question the name? The Fae would know it was true and everyone else would just think they were being cute.

I can't believe I'm thinking they're real. Were Connor's persuasions starting to get to her? "Doesn't the expense of buying it cost you some of your glamarye?"

"Aye, but for my people, 'tis worth it."

"How? I don't get it. How can empty land that no one is allowed to build on be your heritage?"

He smiled. "Well, y'see, 'tis like this. The Fae are spread out all over the world, though we originated here."

"In this valley?"

"Nay, lass, I meant here in Ireland. Anyway, spread out as we are, we've seen the results of pollution and mortals' disregard of the land. This small piece of the Emerald Isle is our heritage for our children. We keep it pristine and natural so that when life becomes too much or we feel a yearnin' to return to the native sod, we have a place we can come to."

"That's a wonderful sentiment," P.J. said. "But do you really think you can keep them out forever?"

"Yes...yes, I do. There's a powerful glamarye upon this valley, one that will allow any of the Fae to pass through, yet mortals may only stand and stare. Oh, they may believe they've visited the valley—'tis a powerful illusion—but as long as there is still magic in the world, this small bit of heaven will be bright and clean and free."

He glanced at her then, as if daring her to try her will against the glamarye set upon the valley.

P.J. couldn't. Connor's words had her completely in his thrall. Though she still had doubts about his magical claims, she couldn't doubt the sincerity and the pride in his voice as he spoke of the responsibility he was entrusted with. He believed so fully, so deeply, she would feel like a jerk if she were to shatter his illusions now.

"You're a remarkable man, Connor O'Flaherty," she said softly.

His answering smile was wistful. "Am I, now?" His green eyes turned cloudy as he peered searchingly into her eyes. "And 'tis times like this I wish I were just that—a mortal man, and not one with all these responsibilities and . . . obligations."

Obligations? Like his obligation to marry only a woman of faerie blood? P.J.'s heart beat an excited rhythm in her chest, but she hesitated to ask it aloud, afraid to know the answer.

Connor turned back to stare out over his people's valley, pride and satisfaction evident in his stance. With a rush of feeling, P.J. realized anew how much she cared for this wonderful man. And, Lord help her, she respected his decision to commit to a relationship only with one of the Fae.

If it was a delusion, it was a mighty consistent one and one others seemed to share, such as Madame Cherelle and Bernard. P.J. had to honor him for sticking to his principles, even if she didn't agree with them.

It hurt though—it hurt knowing that Connor couldn't be more than a brief interlude in her life. Especially since she knew in the deepest, most secret part of herself that there'd never be another man like him.

Her sense of loss fueled defiance. To hell with her scruples. She'd just enjoy the short time they had left together.

P.J. reached up to caress his cheek, and he looked at her, a question in his eyes. She pressed her lips to his, and he responded with an exquisitely gentle kiss.

"Thank you, lass," he said, and squeezed her hand.

She didn't have to ask what he was thanking her for. She knew he was grateful she hadn't tried to prove him wrong by entering the valley—for accepting his claims for once.

They turned as one to the car and headed back toward the small rustic inn nestled in the Irish countryside. Tired from the events of their full day, they elected not to change for dinner and sought out their hostess.

The plump-cheeked matron gave Connor a blinding smile and dropped a small curtsy. "All is as ye asked and ye have the dining room to yerselves tonight."

The woman led them to the dining room and beamed with pride at Connor's pleased look, then hurried off, saying, "I'll not be botherin' ye unless ye call for me."

P.J. glanced around, wholly enchanted by the scene. The dining room was warm and comfortable with rich polished woods and warm tweeds surrounding a central fireplace that looked as though it had been built with native stone. The soft glow of firelight lit the room, echoed in scattered clusters of candles on the tables along the walls.

Eschewing the regular tables, their hostess had placed plump inviting cushions around a low table in front of the fire. Dinner, a plain feast of meat, potatoes and a simple dessert, reposed elegantly on the table next to a bottle of vintage wine. How charming. They were certainly getting the royal treatment tonight.

Royal? "Don't tell me," P.J. said. "Another 'subject' of yours?"

Connor chuckled. "Aye, lass. But don't begrudge her this moment. She'll have a lovely story to tell for years to come, and we get a very nice meal."

P.J. nodded. What more could she ask for? Good food, good wine, wonderful atmosphere... and Connor. She smiled and he led her toward the cushions, pulling her down beside him.

He poured the wine and raised his glass to hers, the firelight leaping in his dark eyes. "To—" he paused, obviously searching for the right words "—success. To finally catching the thief tomorrow."

Disappointed, P.J. murmured, "Tomorrow," and lowered her eyes as she sipped the wine. Knowing he'd promised to have a serious relationship with only one of the Fae, had she really expected him to toast to the two of them?

No, of course not. That afternoon she'd seen clear through to his soul as they overlooked the beautiful valley he'd worked so hard to save for his people. Now she could almost understand his single-mindedness. If he was king of the Fae—and he truly believed he was—then his sense of fair play would let him do nothing less than adhere to what he believed was right for his people.

She just wished she could believe it, too.

P.J. sighed wistfully. Perhaps, tonight, she could just let go of her misgivings and for once enjoy the moment. Connor would undoubtedly catch his thief tomorrow. When he did, their lovely trip would be over, and that would be the last time she'd ever see him. Knowing that, how could she waste their last night together in doubt and mistrust?

"Tell me about your people," she urged.

Connor looked at her in surprise. "My people?"

"Yes, the Fae," P.J. said, and smiled reassuringly. She wanted to know more about those who commanded such devotion from him.

He relaxed, and over their delicious meal he told her about their struggle to retain their dying magic in a disbelieving world, to regain the glory they had once had; how he'd persuaded them to give up clinging to the old ways and move into the twentieth century; and how he agonized over whether he'd done the right thing.

Charmed by his intensity and feeling his frustration, P.J. reached out to lay a soothing hand against his cheek.

Connor groaned softly, his eyes glowing with a savage inner fire as he captured her hand and pressed a lingering kiss against her palm.

Answering passion fired within her, and P.J. inhaled sharply, her breasts tightening beneath the soft outlines of her sweater. No, this was wrong. She'd wanted to get to know him better, not torture the two of them with increased desire. She tugged her hand away, regretting her impulse.

Connor's hungry gaze skimmed her body, catching and holding on to those telltale hardened peaks. He swallowed hard and shifted uncomfortably. P.J.'s breasts tightened even more, until they were almost painful, rigidly pointing at him in insolent demand.

Connor pushed away from the table, his dessert barely touched, and wiped his mouth with the napkin. "I think I'd best be goin' now."

He started to stand, but P.J. leaned over to stop him with a hand on his arm, unwilling to let him leave just yet. "Don't you want your dessert?"

His gaze darted down to where her breast pressed against his arm, and P.J. blushed. She'd meant the sweet, but he obviously thought she meant something else.

Connor's gaze flicked back to her face, as if he didn't want to be caught staring. "No, I couldn't eat another bite," he said, his voice thick.

She released his arm as if it were burning. Damn. She hadn't meant for this to happen. She rose swiftly to move away from him, but her foot caught on a pillow and she stumbled.

His arms caught her and he righted her slowly. For a brief, splendid moment she just stood there, reveling in the feel of his warm, strong body against hers, the scratchy feel of his sweater against her skin and his musky, masculine scent. Embarrassed, she glanced up to apologize, but her voice caught in her throat at the look in his eyes.

Raw, aching need glimmered in his gaze as he molded her body to his and lowered his mouth in a scorching kiss. The world spun, whirling her in dizzying circles of sensation as his tongue thrust urgently into her mouth. Thrilling at the passion she'd innocently unleashed in him, P.J. gave into the temptation of the moment and responded to that soul-shattering kiss.

But despite her battered senses, a small thread of reason remained, dragging her back to awareness. No matter how much she wanted it, this wasn't right.

She tore her lips from his and pulled out of his embrace. "No, Connor, I can't," she said in an agonized wail.

Connor shoved a trembling hand through his hair and turned away. "Aye, lass. You're right. I...I'm sorry."

He inhaled deeply, then turned back to her, smiling. "So tell me, P.J., what's your real name? Punkin? Princess?" His voice was light, teasing, yet somehow intent.

Relieved that Connor was trying to lighten the charged atmosphere, P.J. chuckled. "No, neither of those."

He cocked his head and regarded her steadily. "Why won't you tell me your real name, lass?"

She grinned. "Because I love it when you call me lass."

"No, I'm serious, P.J. Why won't you tell me your real name?"

Her gaze slid away from his probing scrutiny. "I...I...It's embarrassing."

"After what we've shared?" he asked softly.

She still wouldn't meet his gaze. "My name isn't important."

"The devil it isn't!"

Startled at the emotion in his voice, she said, "Wha—"

"You'll give me your body but not your name? Why, P.J.?"

"I don't know...."

"I see. You don't trust me yet. You're still thinking I'm a flake and a phony and you'll not be trusting your name with the likes of me. Is that it?"

She bit her lip, but didn't reply. Unfortunately she knew her answer was plain enough on her guilt-stricken face.

With a muttered, "I'd best be going, then," Connor walked away.

Damn it, she'd given him the benefit of the doubt all night. Couldn't he be content with that?

No, apparently not. Instead, he wanted her to reveal the deepest, most secret part of herself. And what did he offer in return? Nothing.

Damn him—why'd he have to ruin one of their last nights together? With angry tears filling her eyes, P.J. stalked off to her room. If that's the way he wanted to play it, that was fine with her. From now on she'd keep their relationship strictly business. No mere man, no matter how charming, was going to take her emotions on a roller-coaster ride again.

Chapter Nine

Saints be praised, the flight to London was short, mercifully so. P.J. gave Connor the silent treatment: cool, aloof and very unapproachable. He didn't know how to react, especially with so many strangers around, so he just endured it for the length of the trip, wondering what he'd done to deserve it.

Once they finally reached the hotel, P.J. disappeared into the recesses of her room with a freezing silence. Connor stayed in his own room and pretended to read, hoping it would distract him.

It didn't work. He couldn't concentrate and found himself straining for sounds of P.J. through the connecting door. All he could think of was her sitting alone in the next room, doing Lord knows what, and cursing the day she'd met Connor O'Flaherty.

Finally he could stand it no longer. He tossed the book on the bed and strode over to the adjoining door and pounded on it. No response. Where was she?

He pounded more forcefully.

"What d'you want?"

His shoulders sagged in relief when he heard her voice. He checked his watch. It was almost dinner-time. "I'm getting a wee bit hungry," he yelled through the connecting door. "Will you be after havin' dinner with me, lass?"

"I'm not hungry," came the muffled reply.

"But I am, and you should be, too. Come on, lass, you need to keep your strength up," he coaxed.

"I'm fine." Even through the closed door her voice came through clipped and curt.

He lowered his voice so the rest of the hotel wouldn't hear him. "I'll not be letting you stay in there and sulk, y'know. If you don't open this door right now, I'll do it for you."

She jerked open the door and glared at him. "I'm not sulking."

Perhaps not, but she did look tired, as if she'd been indulging in a good pout all day. "Then what *have* you been doing?"

Looking distinctly annoyed, P.J. snapped, "I've been making notes for the article. You know, the one you hired me to write?"

It tore at his heart to see her so prickly and defensive, especially when he was the cause of it. "I know, lass," he said as gently as he could, "but you do need to eat."

All the fight went out of her as she relaxed and heaved a tired sigh. "I suppose, but I don't feel like getting dressed up and going out."

"Why don't we just have dinner in my room, then?"

P.J. gave him a dirty look and Connor cursed his unwary tongue. Why'd he have to remind them both of their previous intimate dinners?

Quickly suppressing his surge of desire at the memory, he resolved to treat P.J. as if she were his younger sister. He put an arm around her shoulders. "Come on, everything will be just fine, and I've an apology to make."

P.J. looked up at him in apprehension. "An apology?"

"Yes, lass." He guided her into the room and pushed her gently down into one of the easy chairs. "But first, food. What would you like to eat?"

She waved her hand listlessly. "Oh, whatever. Nothing heavy."

"How about an omelet, then?"

P.J. nodded, and he called room service to place their order, then came back to sit in the chair across from her.

She regarded him warily. "You're not going to apologize for making love to me, are you?"

He sighed. "No, lass. I'll never regret that, though I could wish it had never happened."

Her mouth twisted in a grimace. "Why? Because I'm not one of the blasted *Fae?*" She made it sound like a dirty word.

"That's the primary reason, yes. You knew when we met that I had responsibilities I couldn't shirk." He brushed her cheek with his fingers, unable to keep from touching her with the simple affectionate gesture. "But 'tis also because now I'll never stop wanting you, never stop longing to kiss your sweet lips, to hold you in my arms."

She glanced up with a bewildered look. "But—"

"But it can't be, I've told you that. I'll not be treatin' you like some common plaything just to satisfy my own desires."

"But I don't—"

"And I can't be making love to a woman who doesn't trust me enough to tell me her name," he interrupted her softly.

P.J. bit her lip, then sighed. "Yes, I understand. But let me tell you my side of it, will you?"

"All right." It seemed a fair enough request.

She squeezed his hand. "Not only is my name embarrassing, it's very private—very important to me. I've never trusted anyone enough to share it, and it's awfully difficult to change a lifetime of secrecy. Only my family knows it, and if it were up to me, they wouldn't know it, either."

He nodded in comprehension and watched as she swallowed hard. "I love my parents, but they betrayed my trust—they lied to me, telling me magic really existed when they knew it didn't." She smiled wryly. "Oh, I know they didn't mean to hurt me, but they did. Now you claim to have a wonderful kind of magic, a magic you haven't been able to prove. Even if I...if I...loved you, how could I trust you?"

Her eyes pleaded for understanding, and unwillingly Connor gave it. Unfortunately, he did understand.

She licked her lips in a strangely nervous gesture. "And then to have you tell me that, even if *you* loved *me,* you could never ask me to marry you...don't you see? That makes me even less inclined to trust you."

Connor ran a hand over his face. She was right. He'd been a fool to expect anything more than she'd already given. Yet, logic be damned, he still yearned to earn her trust.

"I'm sorry, lass. That's why I wanted to apologize. I had no right to touch you. I just wanted—" He wanted her to trust him enough to give her name freely, but he knew better than to ask for that now. "Well, never mind that. I just want to apologize. Can you forgive me?"

P.J. smiled. "All right, just don't do it again."

He couldn't resist teasing her a little. "Thank you... Portia?"

P.J. laughed out loud. "You never give up, do you?"

Connor shook his head. "No, I never do. And to show you how sorry I am, I'd like to give you your very own pair of custom-made Stayle O'Flaherty shoes, on me."

"Oh, no, I couldn't. They're so expensive, and really, it's not necessary."

"Please, I insist. Besides, I'll admit to havin' an ulterior motive. How can I prove to you that magic exists unless you try it for yourself?"

Her look was almost wistful as she said, "All right, I'd like that. Thank you. Can we still be friends?"

He gave her a chaste kiss on the forehead. "Aye, lass, we can." It might kill him, but if that's what she wanted, that's what he'd give her.

THE NEXT MORNING Connor knocked on P.J.'s door and grinned when she opened it. "Top of the mornin' to you, lass."

P.J. laughed. "I didn't know people really said that. You certainly sound chipper."

"Oh, I am, I am." He planted a kiss on her nose. "'Tis the day I've been waitin' for. Today, surely we'll nab our thief."

"That's right—he's your last suspect. But...what if he isn't the one?" She frowned prettily, a crease appearing between her eyebrows.

Connor brushed her misgivings aside and lightly rubbed away the crease. "Nonsense. He must be the one, and you'll not make me believe aught else."

She smiled sadly. "All right, if—when—you prove he's the thief, what are you going to do?"

"The most important thing is to find the talisman. I'll just follow him until I find out where it is, then wait until his attention is drawn elsewhere, grab the shoehorn and we're off."

P.J. chuckled. "You make it sound so easy."

It would be easy. Once he knew the man had the talisman, Connor could use his magic to recover it and incarcerate the thief—a very legitimate use of his power. He glanced at P.J. No, he'd better not explain. After their new understanding, he didn't want to see her face turn stony at the mention of his magic. "Aye, it will be easy. You'll see," he said, and escorted her out of the hotel.

Taking a cab to the theater district, where the Magnificent Ambrose was performing a matinee, they deliberately arrived early so they could see the magician in action and determine if he was using the talisman's magic in his act. As they settled into the seats amid a sea of children and their harried mothers, the lights dimmed and the show began.

The Magnificent Ambrose, a tall, thin man, appeared with an ostentatious bow. His patter was rather uninspired, but as he pulled scarves out of thin air and a Yorkshire terrier out of a hat, Connor realized the act had a bit of pizzazz lacking in many others—a certain spark of... magic.

Connor's eyes narrowed. Was it the influence of Stayle's shoes or Stayle's stolen talisman? He couldn't get a good look at the shoes from here, but as for the other... Connor blurred his vision to see if he could catch the man using stolen magic.

P.J. glanced at him curiously. "What are you doing?"

"I'm tryin' to see if he's using Stayle's talisman."

Several of their neighbors objected to their conversation with loud shushing noises. P.J. leaned closer. "How?" she whispered. "I thought you had true sight."

"Aye, but I mentioned earlier there's a way to see the glamarye everyone else sees. Would you be willing to try it?" Perhaps now she'd be more open-minded.

P.J. looked doubtful, but whispered, "Okay. What do I have to do?"

"Just unfocus your eyes—blur your vision. That's right. Don't look straight at the man, look beyond him."

P.J. followed his directions, squinting up at the stage. "I don't see anything different."

"Nor do I," he admitted. The man wasn't using the talisman as far as he could tell. Then again, Ambrose could use it only if he was one of the Fae. Since he'd failed Stayle's test, he was no such thing, but that didn't mean he didn't have the talisman hidden somewhere. Ambrose had to be their thief—he was the only suspect left. Maybe his assistant was the one with the power.

"Keep watching," Connor advised. "If they use it, 'twill most likely be in the grand finale."

P.J. nodded and continued to squint at the stage.

As the Magnificent Ambrose tapped all four sides of a large box with his wand and asked his pretty assistant to step inside, Connor irreverently wished the man *would* jazz up the act with a little glamarye.

A slow grin spread across his face as an idea occurred to him. Should he? Why not? It wouldn't be very expensive in terms of magic, and he could get a little of his own back on the thief who had given Stayle so much grief. Connor glanced at P.J.'s intent stare. And now, with P.J. finally willing to believe, how could he not use every means at his disposal to get her to trust him?

Connor waited until the magician made his assistant disappear. With a dramatic flourish Ambrose opened the box and his assistant reappeared and emerged, bowing.

Now! Connor muttered a few Gaelic words and sent a surge of power through his talisman ring, squinting his eyes to see the result.

Another woman, twin to the first, emerged and stood next to the assistant and bowed. P.J. gasped and the performers looked startled, but bowed along with the illusory woman as the audience clapped in approval. A man stepped out, the magician's twin, and ranged himself alongside the other three. The magician and his assistant turned white. Their expressions were bewildered, but they gamely bowed when the others did.

Connor had two more sets of doppelgängers trot out, bowing in unison with their duplicates before the joke wore thin and he decided enough was enough. He sent the illusions filing back into the box, making each one disappear in a puff of colored smoke.

The audience laughed and applauded, though Connor didn't miss P.J.'s quickly indrawn breath or the look of shock on the performers' faces.

"Connor," P.J. whispered. "When I crossed my eyes, I saw—"

"Aye, I know. Watch this next one."

Shaken but still game, the Magnificent Ambrose prepared his grand finale—sawing his assistant in half. Grinning, Connor decided the act needed a bit of spice.

The act proceeded as expected until the magician split the box in two. When Ambrose closed the box back together, Connor took control of the illusion.

Suddenly the bottom half fell off the platform. The magician stepped back, startled, as the legs landed on their feet. Connor grinned. It looked like something you'd see in a cartoon: square head, no torso and long, slender legs.

The box scurried frantically around the stage as if seeking its upper half, scanning the audience, peering under the tablecloth and checking behind the curtains. Finally it turned toward the center of the stage and stopped dead. Tilting its "head" slowly upward, it did a double take as if it had finally found what it was searching for.

Ignoring the horrified look on the face of the assistant, the box gave a little bound of satisfaction, then jumped back up to the platform and settled in its accustomed place—upside down.

The audience laughed. With a wiggle and a twitch, the box quickly righted itself and turned over to the proper position. Its relieved sigh echoed through the hall, and the crowd went wild as the harried faces of the performers were mercifully hidden by the closing curtains.

Thunderous applause and cries for an encore echoed throughout the small theater, but none was forthcoming. Eventually realizing the show was at an end, the audience filed out of their seats, laughing and talking.

P.J. and Connor rose to go backstage, and P.J. gave Connor a strange look. "I...I saw it. Two sets of quadruplets...ghostly feet running around. B-but only when I blurred my vision as you showed me." Her voice was full of wonder. "Was he using...real magic?" It was obvious she wanted to believe, yet was afraid to.

"Nay, lass, that was me." He wanted to make sure she knew exactly where the magic was coming from.

"You?" Her tone was incredulous, disbelieving.

Triumph welled within him. Not only had P.J. actually seen his magic, but the thief was almost in his grasp now, too. "Shh," he said as they approached backstage.

The assistant sat with her head between her knees as the magician listened to the hearty congratulations of the theater manager. "Marvelous act, Ambrose, old boy. Simply marvelous. What a farewell performance! Are you sure you won't stay on for a few more weeks? That was the best you've ever done."

The magician shook his head numbly. "No, we . . . we have another engagement—out of town. I can't cancel it, I'm afraid."

"Too bad," the manager said, and slapped him on the back. "Well, next time you're in town, look me up and we'll give it another go, eh?"

The magician nodded and the manager left. When P.J. and Connor stepped out from the wings, the magician gave them a harried look. "I'm sorry—no autographs. I'm not . . . feeling well."

P.J. stepped forward and held out her hand. "We had an appointment, Mr. Ambrose. I'm P. J. Sheridan, the writer."

Ambrose shook her hand, then ran a hand over his face. "Oh, yes, I'd forgotten. I'm sorry, but I'm really in no condition for an interview right now. If you could come back later . . ."

Connor had waited long enough, and he wanted proof of this man's guilt right now. "We came all the way from America to see you. Surely you could grant us a moment of your time."

Connor smiled grimly and stepped forward, thrusting his arm out belligerently. He wasn't above using his size to intimidate the lanky magician into shaking his hand.

Ambrose reached out hesitantly toward Connor's hand, as if he were afraid it would bite—or perhaps jump off and run about the stage a bit.

Connor grinned with triumph and grasped the magician's hand firmly, waiting for the telltale tingling sensation.

Nothing.

Connor's grin faded and he pressed his talisman ring more firmly into the man's hand.

Still nothing.

Ambrose wasn't the thief. How was it possible? Connor dropped the magician's hand and looked at P.J., shaking his head.

P.J.'s eyes widened momentarily, then she reverted to her professional-reporter persona. "It will only take a moment of your time, Mr. Ambrose."

He looked scared, and Connor took pity on him. If he'd known the man was innocent, he would never have messed with his act. "No, lass, tell him who we really are." He favored her with a private wink, hoping she'd follow his lead.

"Why don't you tell him?" she parried, putting the ball back in his court.

"All right," Connor said with a dramatic sigh. "I'm afraid we've used you terribly, Mr. Ambrose. Y'see, we represent a company that is experimenting with a new hologram technology to be used on stage and screen. We used your act to test it—to see if it was ready to market."

The magician looked relieved, and the assistant's head came up slowly, hope shining in her eyes. It appeared she'd much rather believe in holograms than mass delusions. Unfortunately it appeared P.J. felt the same.

Ambrose's face relaxed. "You mean those people, the legs . . . they were holograms?"

"Aye, that they were."

Fear and confusion disappeared, to be replaced by indignation. "Then why the devil didn't you warn us?"

Connor shrugged. "We had to make sure the illusions appeared solid to everyone, even under the closest scrutiny. Did they appear real to you?"

The assistant nodded emphatically. "You betcha. Nearly scared me half to death."

Connor smiled. "I'm sorry about that, but it couldn't be helped."

The magician's chest expanded, and his brow furrowed. To head off the incipient thunderstorm, Connor pulled out his checkbook. "To compensate you for your assistance, involuntary though it was, we'd like you to have this."

He scribbled out a check and handed it to the magician. The assistant peeked at the amount and her eyes widened.

"We're very sorry if we've caused you any distress," Connor said. "Will this take care of it?"

The magician appeared uncertain, but the woman tugged on his arm, whispering urgently. He turned reluctantly back to Connor. "All right, but when you want to market this holo...thing, I want to make sure you give me first crack at getting one...and a discount, too!"

Connor grinned. "I'm not sure it'll be on the market anytime soon, there are a lot of bugs to work out. But if we do, I promise, you'll get one."

They shook hands on it, and Connor escorted a strangely silent P.J. out the side door into the bright sunlight.

She turned to him. "Okay, which is it—magic or hologram?"

Connor couldn't resist. "Surely you know there're no such things as portable moving holograms—they're a myth."

She rolled her eyes. "Why do I bother? I suppose you're saying it's magic?"

"Aye, why do you find it so hard—" He broke off suddenly as he spotted an all-too-familiar face lurking across the street.

Connor pulled P.J. back down the side street they'd just exited.

"What is it?" P.J. demanded.

"Shh," Connor said, and peered around the corner. "Aye, 'twas just as I thought. 'Tis Neil Chalmers."

P.J. flattened her back against the wall and cursed to herself. *Neil Chalmers!* That man kept showing up everywhere they went. Since they'd changed hotels, he'd obviously tracked down the person they were to interview and was lying in wait for them.

Damn the man—couldn't he take a hint? She had absolutely no desire to be in his movie, or to come anywhere near it or him.

Connor tugged on her arm. "I don't think he's seen us. Let's go the other way."

P.J. nodded and followed him out the other end of the street and onto the next block, where they hailed a taxi. She sank into the seat in relief. "Whew! I'm glad we lost him. What a pest."

Connor nodded glumly.

She turned to peer at him more closely. "What's wrong?"

"We're back where we started from. I thought for sure Ambrose would be the thief, but he tested clean."

His mouth twisted into a grimace. "We cleared all the suspects, and I don't have any more leads. I've failed Stayle, and my people." He sounded dejected, forlorn.

P.J. couldn't bear to see him like this. "No, you haven't failed yet. We'll still find Stayle's talisman. You'll see."

"And how will we be doin' that?"

"Well, since you've cleared these five, someone else must have stolen it. We'll just have to go back to Vail and question Stayle more closely about the events of that day."

"But she's already told me everything she knows."

"Maybe, maybe not. Let me have a crack at her." She grinned. "I've got lots of experience as a nosy reporter. If there's any knowledge left to wring out of her, I'll find it." She made her voice sound confident, though she wasn't really all that sure she could keep her promise.

Connor brightened at the hope she offered. "All right, but what about your story? I'm sorry you didn't get your interview with Ambrose." He smacked his palm against his forehead. "Faith! We didn't even get a good look at his shoes."

P.J. shrugged. "It doesn't matter. I have almost enough information to write an article, anyway."

"Almost? What is it you're missin'?"

"After that demonstration in the theater, I . . . I'm almost convinced you have real magic," she whispered, not wanting the driver to hear.

"But not quite?"

"No, I need a little more evidence—more proof, so I can be sure it really was magic and not a hologram. Your explanation to Ambrose was far too plausible."

Connor frowned. "I told you I promised to use my magic only when 'twas absolutely necessary."

She raised a disbelieving eyebrow. "Like the magician's act?"

His ears reddened. "Well, that was different, y'see. I...I thought the man was the thief, and that I could trip him up, get him to reveal his true nature. Besides, 'twas only glamarye, not the lasting sort of magic you'll be wantin' to see."

"No, if you show me glamarye, and convince me that's what it is—a part of your magic—I'll take your word for the rest of it."

Connor gave her a lopsided grin. "All right, then." He asked the driver to stop the car about two blocks from their hotel, and they exited on Regent Street in the midst of a crowd of shoppers.

Connor rubbed his hands together. "All right, lass. What'll it be? You name it so you'll know I've not rigged it ahead of time."

P.J. glanced around, considering. Across the street, a lingerie-shop window displayed a mannequin sitting on a satin-covered bed, wearing nothing but a long black wig and a lacy red teddy. "There—make that mannequin come to life."

Connor grinned. "All right, watch. And don't forget to squint your eyes."

P.J. obediently blurred her vision and watched the shop window as people hurried past. A fuzzy outline took shape around the mannequin, and it soon took on softer, more human features.

Familiar features.

P.J.'s features.

She gasped. "Connor, what are you doing?"

He grinned. "Well, with that long black hair and all, I thought she looked a wee bit like you. Watch."

P.J. turned to stare in horror as the mannequin stretched and yawned. People, mostly men, began to stop and watch the window. The mannequin smiled and waggled her fingers at them.

Is that how P.J. looked to Connor? She felt her face turn hot. The vision was altogether too flattering. P.J.'s skin wasn't all that translucent, nor her face that exotic and alluring. Connor must have one hell of an imagination.

The gathering crowd blocked her vision, and P.J. tugged at Connor's sleeve. "Put it back. Now!"

Connor nodded and complied. Through a momentary gap in the throng, P.J. saw her twin sit up and blend into the plastic mannequin, until the face blurred back into the rigid features.

The crowd watched for another moment or two, then dispersed. About half of them entered the lingerie store, and the other half went back to their shopping, talking excitedly among themselves. One old gent spotted P.J., recognition dawning on his face. "Say there, wasn't that you—"

P.J. grabbed Connor's arm. "Let's get out of here!"

Connor laughed and used his bulk to weave a way through the crowd for them, never stopping until they reached the safety of their hotel lobby and were sure no one had followed them.

"So, lass. Did you get your proof?"

"Yes, I did, but you sure picked a fine way to..." Her voice trailed off as she realized what she'd just said.

Yes, she *had* gotten her proof. There was no way Connor could've staged that. He couldn't know when or where she'd ask him to demonstrate his glamarye, and it was quite evident that at least ten other people had seen the same thing she had. No, make that a hundred other people, if you counted the stage illusions. She believed him now.

Magic was real!

Her world tilted and reformed anew. The accompanying wave of realization made her giddy with elation. She grabbed Connor's lapel for support and closed her eyes until the dizziness passed. She opened them again to gaze into his twinkling green eyes.

"I told you I'd help you find your magic," he whispered.

She laughed. Everything was so much brighter, so much sharper and clearer. It was as if a mist had been obscuring her vision for years and had suddenly vanished, needing only her belief in magic. In its place was a truer, more vivid awareness of the world.

P.J. threw her arms around Connor's neck and kissed him enthusiastically. "Yes, isn't it wonderful?"

Connor grinned and gave her a hug, then steered her toward the elevator. "Aye, that it is, but we'll be needin' to pack our bags now if we're to catch tonight's flight to the States and avoid Neil Chalmers."

Once alone in her hotel room, P.J. hugged the knowledge to herself. Magic was real! And her beloved Connor was one of the magic wielders. It was wonderful... or was it?

The elation slowly faded, and in its place was left...emptiness. Why did she feel this way? Now that she knew magic really did exist, she should be overjoyed. After all, she'd finally accomplished her goal.

Her goal. That was it—the quest for magic had consumed her entire life. Now that she'd found it, what was left? She felt adrift, rudderless. And that wasn't the worst part. In her dreams of discovering real magic, she'd always assumed that once she found it, it would be only a matter of learning how it worked, then using it herself.

That's why she felt so low. She'd found real magic, all right, but only those with faerie blood could use it. Save for a massive transfusion—and what faerie in its right mind would go for that?—magic was forever beyond her reach.

No, the only way she could experience magic was through Connor.

And he was slated for a faerie woman.

Chapter Ten

As Connor drove from the airport, all P.J. wanted to do was go home and rest. She'd been elated once he'd cleared Ambrose of suspicion and she realized their quest would keep them together a little longer, but the proof of his magic had changed all that.

She'd tried to sort through what had happened and what it meant to her, but she hadn't been able to think with Connor around. All she knew was that her world had turned upside down and she needed time to think about it—away from him and his distracting presence.

Connor stopped at her apartment and carried her suitcase to the door. She turned to tell him goodbye, but he wore a stubborn look that told her he wasn't going to leave until he saw the inside of her apartment.

She sighed. Why not? He knew her by now, knew her more intimately than most people. Since she hadn't told him her real name, she might as well let him see another small piece of her. She handed him her key in a gesture of surrender and he opened the door, ushering her inside.

She turned on the light and paused. How would he see it? The living room was small and cramped, the tiny couch in front of the television fighting for space with the army-surplus desk and filing cabinets of her profession. Papers spilled over every available surface, and the walls were covered with photographs of the many subjects she'd interviewed over the years, interspersed with framed articles with her byline. It was more of an office than a living room—not exactly the ideal place to entertain a guest.

Connor looked around in silence, then smiled. "Yes, this reminds me of you—all professional and aloof on the outside, but the inside..."

"The inside?"

"I'll bet..." He took the few steps to her bedroom door and opened it.

P.J. knew what he'd see there—the room was decorated in soft floral pastels, with light, airy furniture. It was the one place she allowed her whimsical side to show through.

He nodded and smiled at her. "Aye, 'tis as I thought. The inside is warm and soft and feminine just like you."

Why had she worried? She should have known Connor would understand. She gave him a tender, tired smile.

"Ah, but you'll be that weary, and here I am blathering on. Tomorrow will be soon enough for us to talk to Stayle. I'll be picking you up around noon so you can get some rest, all right?"

P.J. nodded. Right now all she wanted was to go to bed and rest her fatigued brain.

Connor placed her suitcase in the bedroom, kissed her on the forehead and murmured his goodbyes. He let himself out and P.J. lay down on the bed, promising herself to rest for just a moment before she tackled the chore of unpacking. Instead she fell fast asleep.

P.J. HEARD A KNOCK at her door and opened it, smiling at Connor. It'd only been a few hours, but she already missed him—missed his ready humor, his slow, dimpled smile and those laughing green eyes. Now seeing him anew, she realized how lucky she was to be with him, if only for a short time. This man could have anyone he wanted—he was magic, in more ways than one.

Connor caught her up in a big bear hug. "I missed you," he said simply.

"Me, too." She felt safe and warm and loved. Everything would be just fine, she knew it.

An hour later she wasn't so sure.

Stayle muttered and paced the length of her boutique's showroom, closed to the public until the talisman was found. She looked haggard and wan. Turning on Connor, she said, "What d'you mean, you haven't found me talisman? You've been off gallivantin' all over the world, and with what t'show fer it?" She gestured mockingly at P.J. "Nothing but an infatuated mortal, it looks like. I warned you about that, y'know."

P.J. kept silent and Connor came to her defense. "My relationship with P.J. is none of your concern, and I'll not be havin' you sharpen your tongue on her." He turned to P.J. and lowered his voice. "She usually isn't like this. 'Tis the loss of her talisman that's done it. She can't help it, y'see.''

P.J. nodded in understanding, though she thought privately that Stayle could use some lessons in manners.

Stayle frowned. "Never mind her. What about me talisman? Are you prepared to use your magic to find it now?"

"No," Connor explained with far more patience than P.J. would've had in a similar situation. "My month isn't up yet, and we want to make sure we've exhausted all leads."

Stayle rolled her eyes in exasperation. "And what leads will those be? I told ye everything I know!"

Connor made a conciliatory gesture with his hands. "Maybe. Maybe not. P.J. here is a fine reporter and has a great deal of experience in investigations like this. Let her ask you some questions."

Stayle folded her arms and glared at P.J. "And what do you know about finding a magic talisman, mortal?" she challenged.

P.J. forced herself to reply calmly. This was Connor's sister, whom he obviously loved even when she was being driven bonkers by the loss of her talisman. Ignoring Stayle's challenge, P.J. said, "Let's go over what happened again to see if we can find anything new."

Stayle's lips hardened into a firm line, then opened to utter what P.J. was sure would be a scathing reply.

Connor grasped his sister's shoulder. "She's only trying to help, Stayle, and you're not making things easier. Now answer the lass's questions."

Thus appealed to, Stayle reluctantly cooperated and recited the events of the day. She slapped the records down on the counter. "If you don't believe me, look at the records. There were only five customers that day in the fittin' room, and you've cleared the lot of 'em."

Patiently, P.J. prodded, "Were there any other customers who might have entered the room who didn't purchase the custom-made shoes?"

"No!"

"Tradesmen, perhaps, selling something?"

"No, I told you—"

"Children, relatives of the customers?"

"No, there wasn't..." Stayle paused in thought. "Wait. There was someone else." She grabbed the records in front of her. "Shaughnessy—he brought his wife. And the actress had a man with her."

"A man?" P.J. exchanged a glance with Connor. Was he thinking what she was thinking?

Connor's eyes narrowed as he focused on his sister. "Was he about P.J.'s height, fortyish, with light brown hair?"

Stayle frowned in thought. "Aye, that he was."

"Neil Chalmers," P.J. and Connor said in unison.

Stayle's eyes widened in sudden hope. "Do ye know him?"

Connor grimaced. "Aye, we know him."

P.J. regarded Connor incredulously. "You mean, in all the times we've run into him, you've never touched his hand?"

Connor's eyes narrowed as he thought about it. "No, I haven't. Each time we met, Neil held a drink, a bandage or something so he couldn't shake hands. Very clever."

"You think it was deliberate?"

"It had to be—'twould be too much of a coincidence otherwise."

"But how would he know to avoid your hand?"

"I don't—" Connor broke off and snapped his fingers. "Remember when we interviewed Melissa? The maid left us alone downstairs and we talked about the power of the shoehorn. Then later Neil came out of the side alcove. I'll bet—"

"He was listening! He overheard us saying how we could identify the thief by shaking his hand. No wonder he avoided it." P.J. paused, thinking. "So why has he been following us all over the world? Obviously not to pester me for a part in his film."

"Nay, lass, I'll wager he's trying to figure out how to use the talisman."

"You're right, and that's why he pumped me for so much information on magic." She grinned at him. "He didn't get much."

Stayle, who had been following the conversation with a perplexed look on her face, interrupted. "Does this mean ye know who has me talisman?" she demanded of her brother.

"Aye, we're fairly certain."

"Then go and get it!"

"Not so fast," Connor cautioned. "I thought Ambrose was the thief and it turned out he wasn't. I'm almost positive Neil is, but I want to verify it before I scare him off and he runs and hides somewhere we'll never find him. The world is obviously his playground."

"So go get him, then."

Connor grinned wryly. "'Tisn't that easy. We've been deliberately avoiding him. 'Twould look a mite suspicious right now if we all of a sudden started seekin' out his company."

"But, Connor, if ye know where me talisman is—"

Connor made a shushing motion with his hands. "Quit your blatherin' for a moment and let me think. If he's still looking for us, he's likely to show back up in Vail. He knows we were coming back here. We can't count on that, though. Since we've been avoiding him, he may think we're on to him."

P.J. had an idea. She didn't like it, but if it would help locate the talisman and get this over with, she'd use it. "Connor? Remember when you took Melissa's picture?" He nodded. "Well, you told her you'd give her copies of the photographs once they were developed—"

Connor grabbed her and kissed her, swinging her around. "That's it, lass—a wonderful idea. The pictures should be ready to pick up by now. I'll just take them by and find out where Neil is and what he's doing."

He started out the door, then turned back. "Wait, I almost forgot the shoes I promised you. Stayle, would you give P.J. your client questionnaire, please?"

"What? You're giving her a pair of me shoes, gratis? Why?"

"Do you need to ask?" he said quietly.

Surprisingly, Stayle quailed under the censorious look in his eyes and went into the other room. When she came back, she shoved a sheaf of papers at P.J.

"Here. Ye need to fill these out—honestly, mind you."

Connor scowled, but P.J. touched his arm lightly to reassure him, then thanked Stayle and took the papers.

As they walked out of the boutique, P.J. sighed in relief. Dealing with Connor's sister was rather like confronting a woman with permanent PMS. For the first time in her life P.J. was grateful for her own sister; Stayle made Amaranth look positively normal.

MELISSA'S MAID ushered P.J. and Connor into the white living room of Melissa's condo, then left to inform the actress of their presence. Once the maid was out of sight, P.J. kept watch on the stairs as Connor silently checked out the alcove Neil had emerged from the last time they were there.

Coming back to stand beside P.J., Connor whispered, "'Tis a bathroom, and I'll wager Neil hid in there and listened to everything we said."

P.J. nodded, then shushed him as she heard movement above them. They turned to see Melissa descending the staircase.

"Ms. Sheridan and Mr. Michaels," Melissa said politely. "How nice to see you again. Please, won't you come in and sit down?"

They sat opposite Melissa as she said, "Now, what can I do for you?"

Connor gestured with the folder in his hand. "Here are the pictures I promised you."

Melissa smiled. "Wonderful! Let's see them," she said, and moved to sit next to Connor on the couch.

Ignoring the stab of jealousy that lanced through her, P.J. forced herself to endure the sight of another woman leaning so close to Connor. She supposed she should be grateful Melissa wasn't faerie. Then she'd really have something to worry about.

"Uh, is Mr. Chalmers here?" P.J. asked. She and Connor had agreed on the way over that she'd play the eager aspiring actress as a ploy to learn Neil's whereabouts.

Melissa looked puzzled. "Neil? No, I haven't seen him in quite a while. Why?"

"He said he wanted to use me in his film, and I thought if he was serious..." She allowed her voice to trail off and plastered a suitably stagestruck look on her face.

"I'm sorry," Melissa said. "I don't know where he is. He only shows up every few days or so. The last time I saw him he said he was going to do some research on magic for the film. He'll probably be back tomorrow."

P.J. tried to look dejected. Research? That gave her an idea. She glanced down at the coffee table where Melissa and Connor were sorting through pictures. "Are there any pictures of him in there? I...I'd like to have one."

Connor looked surprised, but nodded. "Yes, I think he ended up in one or two shots." He sorted through them and pulled one out that had a good view of Neil's face. "Will this do?"

P.J. nodded and marked time as Melissa and Connor pored over the pictures. Finally P.J. couldn't take it anymore. She glanced at her watch. "Uh-oh, we'd better be going or we'll be late for our next interview."

Realizing she had to ensure Neil didn't learn of their visit, P.J. turned to Melissa with feigned embarrassment and pleading eyes. "I hate being a pest, but would you please not tell Mr. Chalmers I was here? I...I don't want him to think I'm a star-struck groupie or anything."

With a pitying look in her eyes, Melissa agreed, making P.J. feel guilty. She really had no reason to be jealous of the actress, even if Melissa was drop-dead gorgeous. In fact, P.J. could almost like her.

When P.J. and Connor were finally alone in the car, Connor turned to her. "Well, we didn't learn anything, but you've got an idea, haven't you, lass? I could see those wheels turning a mile a minute."

P.J. chuckled. "Yes, I do. If Neil is doing research on magic in Vail, then no matter where he starts, I have a hunch he'll end up at The Cosmic Connection."

P.J.'S HUNCH WAS RIGHT. Amaranth leaned over the counter, peering at Neil's photo. "Yes, I remember him."

Amaranth had actually come down out of the clouds long enough to notice something? Amazing. P.J.'s spirits sank as she shared a disappointed look with Connor. "Darn, I was hoping he hadn't been here yet."

"Oh, he'll be back," Amaranth assured her.

"How do you know?"

Amaranth shrugged. "He said so."

"Why? Does he know you're my sister?" It was the only explanation she could come up with.

"Oh, no. At least I don't think so."

"Then how do you know he's coming back?"

"Because he said so," Amaranth repeated patiently.

P.J. rolled her eyes. This could go on forever. "Do you know *why* he's coming back?"

Amaranth nodded complacently. "Yes, of course."

P.J. glared at Connor, who seemed to find their conversation vastly amusing. Heroically, she restrained herself from heaving a sigh. "All right, *why* is he coming back?"

"To pick up a book he ordered."

Now they were getting somewhere. "Do you know when he's coming by?"

"Sometime this afternoon."

How strange. Amaranth usually didn't remember anything about her customers, let alone this much detail. "Why do you remember so much about this man?"

Amaranth frowned. "He wasn't very nice—he treated me like an idiot."

P.J. was speechless. To tell the truth, she'd often treated Amaranth that way herself, though she knew her sister was no such thing. In fact, P.J. was doing it now.

Connor smiled at Amaranth and filled in the resulting silence. "That's our boy. Now, lass, do you remember what he was looking for?"

Amaranth smiled, blooming under Connor's attention and charm. "Oh, yes. He wanted to know about objects with magical powers. We didn't have anything in stock, so I ordered a book from Denver on talismanic magic.''

P.J. shared a significant glance with Connor. Neil was beginning to look more and more guilty. And Connor had gotten more out of Amaranth with a smile than P.J. had in twenty agonizing minutes of questions. She had to remember his technique. For now she'd let him handle the rest of the questioning.

"Will you be doing us a favor then, lass?"

"Sure," Amaranth said without hesitation. "What is it?"

Connor leaned forward confidingly. "We need to meet the man, without making it obvious we're looking for him. If we go upstairs to your sister's office, could you let us know, on the sly, when he comes in? That way we can come down and run into him, accidental-like."

Amaranth considered for a minute. "Are you going to do something bad to him?"

Connor gave her an honest answer. "We think he may have stolen something from my sister. This'll help us find out. If so, yes, we'll see he gets just what he deserves."

Amaranth smiled. "Good. I'm sure he's your thief. He gave me such bad vibes, I had to do a spiritual cleansing of the store after he left."

Connor nodded as if Amaranth made perfect sense. Come to think of it, maybe she did. P.J.'s notions of what was real magic and what wasn't had been exploded recently, and she wasn't sure of anything anymore.

Amaranth frowned. "But how am I going to signal you?"

"The buzzer," P.J. reminded her. "Remember, I had a button installed beneath the counter so you could buzz me whenever you need me to fill in for you at the counter."

"Oh, that's right," Amaranth said with a marked lack of enthusiasm. Neither she nor their parents liked the intrusion of technology in their domain and refused to use it. Instead they preferred to yell up the stairs—so unprofessional.

Amaranth paused, staring off into space with a distracted look on her face. "You know—"

P.J. hurried to cut her off. *Oh Lord, cosmic fruit here we come.* Amaranth probably had some wild and highly improbable method of telepathy or clairvoyance she wanted to try. "This is the only method we *know* will work, we don't have the time to try anything untested and we do want to make sure we catch the man."

Amaranth looked doubtful. P.J. thought her cause was lost until Connor stepped in to second her. "Good idea. If the man knows magic, he may be able to detect its use, but a prosaic, mundane buzzer...why, he'll never think of that."

Amaranth smiled. "All right, I'll do it." She shooed them out. "Now go on upstairs and I'll buzz you when he comes."

They made themselves comfortable in the office and Connor chuckled. "Now I know why you're such a good reporter."

"Oh? Why's that?"

"Because you've had lots of experience eliciting answers from Amaranth—one of the toughest subjects I've ever seen."

P.J. smiled wryly. "Maybe, but you got far more out of Amaranth with just a smile than I did with ten questions. How do you do it?"

He shrugged. "A lot of the Fae are just like her. By the way, what time does the store close?"

"At five o'clock." She glanced at her watch. "We have a couple of hours to kill—would you like to play a game?"

Connor's gaze turned wry and he quirked a smile at her. Good grief, what did he think she meant?

Quickly she said, "This game is called Revenge. The winner is the person who comes up with the most creative and fitting way of making Neil pay for his crime."

Connor grinned and entered heartily into the spirit of the game. After entertaining each other with wilder and more fanciful schemes, they finally settled on their own preferences.

P.J. favored locking Neil up in a room alone with an angry Stayle, figuring that would be punishment enough for any man. Connor disagreed, fearing the punishment would be too swift. Instead, he leaned toward calling in foul-tempered boggarts—meddling gnomes—to pester Neil to death.

They had finally come to an agreement to give Neil to Stayle *after* the boggarts were done with him when Amaranth came walking in the door. P.J. checked her watch. "Damn. It's after five. Neil didn't show up."

"Oh, no," Amaranth assured her. "He came."

"He did? Why didn't you press the buzzer?" Damn. P.J. should have known better than to trust Amaranth with anything technological.

Amaranth wore a slight frown of indignation. "I did, but you didn't come. You were probably talking so much, you didn't hear it."

That was hardly likely. The noise from that buzzer would wake the dead—or Amaranth from a trance. It's one reason P.J. had selected it. "Now, Amaranth—"

"Let's just check the buzzer, shall we?" Connor interrupted.

P.J. agreed reluctantly. He didn't know Amaranth like she did. Chances were, her sister had *thought* about pressing the buzzer, and for her the thought was as good as the deed. But if it made him happy...

They trooped downstairs and Connor squatted down to take a look at the button underneath the cash register. He poked at it for a moment, then looked up at them. "Aye, here's your problem, the wire seems to have worked itself loose. That's why the buzzer wasn't working."

Mortified, P.J. gave Amaranth an apologetic look.

Amaranth stared back with a stubborn set to her chin. "You should have done it my way."

P.J. deserved that. "You're probably right."

Amaranth looked surprised and pleased. Connor gave P.J. a pleased nod. "Well, it can't be helped. We'll just have to try and find another way to run into Neil."

Amaranth smiled. "Oh, no problem. He left a note."

P.J. groaned. "You didn't tell him we were looking for him, did you?" She grimaced at her own automatic reaction. Amaranth wasn't as flighty as she looked and she deserved to be treated better.

"No, of course not."

"Good, I knew you wouldn't." P.J. was rewarded by beaming smiles from both her sister and Connor. "Would you please tell us exactly what happened?"

"Sure. I gave him the book and pressed the buzzer, but you didn't come down." Amaranth managed to look disapproving and smug at the same time. "I thought you might be a little slow, so I talked to him."

"Good," P.J. encouraged. "You tried to stall him for us. And then?"

"He asked if there was anyone else in Vail who knew a lot about magic. I mentioned your name and told him you were my sister." Amaranth frowned. "Was that okay? You didn't say I couldn't say that."

"That's just fine," P.J. said. "I just didn't want him to know we were looking for him."

Amaranth brightened. "That's okay, then. When I told him I'd be seeing you later, he asked me to give you a note." She pulled a piece of paper out of the pocket of her voluminous skirt. "Here it is."

P.J. smiled at her sister and took the note. "Thank you, Sis. You did just right. Now let's see what Neil has to say."

She scanned the note quickly as Connor looked on in impatience. "Hmm. He actually apologizes for being such a pest . . . says he wants to make it up to both of us." She looked up in surprise. "He's invited us up to one of the huts for the weekend. Says he won't take no for an answer."

Connor looked puzzled. "Huts?"

"They're a series of isolated cabins built high in the mountains. You can rent them out as a base to do some backcountry skiing, or ski from hut to hut. I've never been to one, but the scenery is supposed to be breathtaking."

"Sounds a mite suspicious to me. I wonder what he'll be wanting?"

Conscious of Amaranth's interest, P.J. decided to find some place where she and Connor could talk privately. She didn't want to have to explain this complicated business to her sister, especially when P.J. had a hard time taking it all in herself. "Well, thanks, Amaranth." She gave her sister a sincere hug. "We really appreciate what you've done."

Amaranth seemed to open like a blossom in the sun, and P.J. vowed to give her sister more compliments in the future. "Unfortunately, we have to get going."

Connor leaned over to capture Amaranth's hand and give her one of his Irish blessings. "'As sure as there are leprechauns to make a wish come true, 'tis nothing but the happiest of days I'm wishing you.'" His eyes twinkled with mischief as he smiled engagingly at her. "It was nice meeting you, Amaranth."

Oh, no, P.J. wasn't about to give him the chance to explain that to Amaranth, or they'd never get out of there. Turning to her beaming sister, P.J. said, "Give Mom and Dad a kiss for me, okay?"

"Sure. Oh, I forgot. Did you borrow my snowflake? I can't find it anywhere."

Connor raised an amused eyebrow, and P.J. glanced at the counter where the large crystal paperweight usually sat. It wasn't there, but Amaranth had probably used it elsewhere in the shop and had forgotten it. "Don't worry," P.J. said, "I'm sure it'll turn up soon."

Amaranth nodded and let them out of the shop into the cold biting wind. P.J. shivered and drew her jacket tighter around her face.

Connor joined her outside. "And where is it we're going, lass?"

"Oh, anywhere—back to the car. I just didn't want to explain everything to Amaranth and I thought it best we talk in private about Neil's invitation."

He nodded. "Aye, and I'm not so sure we should be accepting it."

"Why not? He asked us to meet him tomorrow. You probably won't get an earlier chance to touch his hand."

Connor frowned. "Perhaps not, but I'll not be trustin' the likes of him."

P.J. hugged his arm. "Now what could he do that a big strong guy like you, with magic on his side, couldn't handle?"

"I don't know. That's what's bothering me."

"Ah, come on, Connor," she cajoled. "Think about the opportunity to catch the thief who's stolen your sister's talisman. Isn't that worth a little risk?"

"To me, perhaps, but not to you." He turned to grasp her shoulders and look down into her eyes. "All right, I'll go, but you'll be stayin'."

Oh, no, P.J. had just as much right to be in on the denouement as Connor. She'd chased false leads all over the world, too, and had been just as annoyed by Neil as Connor had been. She deserved the chance to be there to unmask the thief. Fleetingly, she recalled Madame Cherelle's prediction of danger in the mountains, but dismissed it instantly. If she reminded Connor of that, he'd never agree to let her go.

Besides, Madame had also said she'd also find her greatest joy, and what could happen with Connor there to protect her? She shook her head decisively. "Wrong. I'm going whether you are or not, so you'd better just make up your mind to it."

Changing her tone, she said, "Come on, Connor, it'll be fun. After we truss Neil up and you zap him off to the boggarts, we'll have the hut all to ourselves. We deserve a little vacation, don't we?" And since it would be the last time she ever saw him, she wanted to ensure the memory was a pleasant one.

Connor nodded, obviously reluctant. "All right, I can't stop you. But if there's any danger, any danger at all, I'll be sending you on your way. Agreed?"

P.J. nodded and grinned. "Agreed."

Chapter Eleven

The next day Connor parked at the store in Vail where Neil had asked them to meet him. It figured—he was late. Electing to stay inside the car where it was still warm, Connor glanced at P.J. doubtfully. "Are you sure this is such a good idea, lass?"

P.J. grinned at him. "Of course it is. Besides, you have to give me a chance to earn the shoes Stayle is making for me. You'll see—with your magic and my investigative skills, what could go wrong?"

Aye, that was the rub. His magic. P.J. still hadn't trusted him with her real name. Without it, he couldn't perform any lasting magic on her—nothing that would affect her in an enduring way. That would make it difficult to protect her if the need arose.

Luckily he'd looked up Neil's full name, just in case. Though he styled himself as Neil Chalmers, Connor hadn't been at all sure that was the man's real name, especially since he was in the movie business. Surprisingly it was the name he was born with: Neil Joseph Chalmers. Connor had resisted the urge to look up P.J.'s name, as well, still hoping she'd tell him of her own accord.

P.J. must have taken Connor's silence as consent, for she turned back to the brochure she'd been reading on the hut system.

"Don't tell me you've lived here all of your life and you don't know any more about the huts than I do," he teased.

Without looking up, she waved her hand dismissive. "Oh, I've heard of them, but I'm not much of a skier, so I never paid much attention. It says here that the Tenth Mountain Division Hut System runs them."

She suddenly stopped and peered closer. "It also says we need to have someone proficient in avalanche awareness, medical emergencies, rescue, bivouac and route finding." She glanced up with a worried look. "Do you know this stuff?"

Connor shrugged. "Some of it. But I'm sure Neil wouldn't have invited us if he didn't."

"Hmm," P.J. answered absently as she continued to read the brochure. "Oh, no!"

"What is it, lass?"

"Did you know these trails don't allow mechanized or motorized transport?"

"No, but it makes sense, so skiers can go from hut to hut without havin' to worry about running into vehicles."

"But I can't—" P.J. broke off, biting her lip.

"You can't what?"

"I . . . I can't imagine how we're going to get there. There's no snow, and as far as I know, none is due until Monday."

"Why, I imagine we'll walk."

She turned the brochure over to examine the map and groaned. "Walk!" she wailed. "Do you realize how far it is to some of these huts? Lord, I hope it's one of the close ones.''

"Are you havin' second thoughts, then?"

"No, I just hadn't planned on walking that far and carrying a suitcase, too."

"Don't worry about it. I'll test him right away. If he's the thief, we won't need to make this trip, anyway."

She nodded and glanced out of the car window. "There's Neil now."

P.J. was determined to go along with this mad scheme, even though she'd made it clear she wasn't at all comfortable with the physical aspects of it. Well, he'd just have to make it as easy on her as possible, and try to get it over with quickly enough so they could get the talisman and go. In fact, why not get it over with now?

Connor exited the car and approached Neil, who was opening the trunk of his car. This time Connor was going to shake the man's hand if he had to chase him down to do it.

Connor strode swiftly up to Neil and stuck his hand out, saying, "It's good to see you, pal." Neil could hardly avoid shaking it without a damn good excuse or outright rudeness. And Connor assumed Neil would avoid rudeness since he'd been trying so hard to get them to come along.

Neil looked startled. He glanced down at his own gloved hand, then extended it hesitantly to shake Connor's.

Connor grinned inwardly in triumph and grasped Neil's hand firmly. If the producer had handled

Stayle's talisman, Connor should be able to feel it even through the thick suede of the glove.

Connor waited for the tingle that would identify Neil as the thief.

Nothing but a bit of discomfort. Saints preserve us, the man's hand was as hard as a rock. Who would've thought it? Connor pressed harder.

Neil gave him a strange look at the prolonged grip and Connor reluctantly let go. There was something odd about that handshake, though he couldn't quite put his finger on what bothered him. Connor wasn't yet convinced that Neil was cleared, but there was no way to test it, short of demanding the man take his gloves off or wrestling him to the ground to do it for him.

If Neil wasn't the thief, that would be very embarrassing, with the potential of leading to a lawsuit for assault. No, Connor would just bide his time and wait for the man to take his gloves off himself. After all, he couldn't wear them all weekend, now could he? And Connor had waited this long; he could wait a little longer, just to make sure.

P.J. joined them, casting a questioning glance at Connor. He could almost read her mind: *Is he guilty?*

Connor shrugged, and P.J. looked exasperated. He knew how she felt—he felt the same.

"Hello, Neil," she said.

Neil smiled. "I'm glad you accepted my invitation. I know I've been persona non grata to you two, but I'll make it up to you—I even booked all the rooms at the Shrine Mountain Inn hut so we won't have any company. Have you ever been in one?"

They shook their heads.

"Good, you have a treat in store for you, then."

P.J. looked a little doubtful. "I was reading up on the hut system, and it says most people ski to them."

Neil laughed. "Yes, I've skied the trails many times, but you can walk them, too. That's what we'll be doing."

P.J. didn't look reassured. "So you know all about avalanches and trail finding and that other stuff they said we have to know?"

"Sure, I'm a regular here. But don't worry, we won't need it. No snow's expected until Monday. We'll be back way before then."

"How far are we going to have to walk?"

"It's just under three miles from the Vail Pass trailhead. I chose that hut because it's the easiest trail to hike."

P.J. nodded and Connor could see the thoughts flicker across her face. She must have decided she could handle three miles. "Okay, but what about our suitcases?"

Neil gestured toward the trunk of his car. "Just in case you were neophytes, I brought all the supplies we'll need, and some backpacks, too. They're a lot easier to carry than suitcases. No sense in taking two cars, so why don't you get your gear and transfer it to my car so we can get going? We'll wait until we get to Vail Pass to distribute the pack loads."

Connor glanced at P.J. to ensure she was serious about going. She nodded, and he went to get their suitcases from the car.

Neil's trunk was fairly full with the supplies, extra backpacks and other strange odds and ends, but they managed to make the suitcases fit.

The ride to Vail Pass was a long thirty minutes as Connor listened with half an ear to Neil's babbling about the beauty of the mountain scenery they were about to experience. When that subject palled, Neil expounded on his film project. Luckily he didn't seem to need any response. An occasional grunt seemed to suffice to keep the man going...and going...and going.

Finally they reached Vail Pass and parked near the trailhead. Neil refused all help in getting the things out of the trunk and advised them on what they should take with them and what they should leave behind. He added the bedrolls and supplies, distributing them evenly among the three packs.

During the entire operation he never took his gloves off, making Connor even more convinced that Neil was the thief. But then, Connor had been wrong before. He winced, embarrassed at the memory of the tricks he'd played on the poor unsuspecting magician. This time he'd make sure Neil was the thief before he took any action.

P.J. looked doubtful as Connor helped her on with her pack and attached the bedroll.

"Can you handle this all right, lass? I'll take some of your load if you want. I'm strong as an ox."

P.J. shook her head. "No, I want to pull my own weight. Don't worry, I can handle it."

Concern for P.J. warred with his agreement to forgo using magic unless it was absolutely necessary. Concern won. P.J.'s health was more important than the small amount of gold a spell would take. Besides, keeping them both alert and untired might be important in dealing with Neil—if he was the thief.

Connor lowered his voice. "There's no sense in makin' this any more difficult than it has to be. What do you say I use a wee bit of magic to make the load feel lighter? I'll do the same for myself," he hurried to add so she wouldn't be stubborn.

"Okay," P.J. whispered. "But don't you dare lighten Neil's."

Connor chuckled, and under pretense of adjusting P.J.'s straps, he called on his power to make her pack feel one-fifth its actual weight, so it was no heavier than that briefcase she lugged around all the time. While he was at it, he lightened his own, as well. No sense wasting a good spell when he'd already used up the gold.

P.J. gingerly tested the weight. "That's great. Thanks."

Neil slammed the trunk closed. "Everyone ready?"

They nodded and he handed them both knit caps. "Here, you're going to need these," he said as he pulled on one of his own.

Well, Neil might be a pest and a thief, but he was certainly prepared for this trip. Connor was impressed. If the man was this organized, maybe he was as good a producer as he claimed.

Neil led the way up the trail, followed by P.J., with Connor bringing up the rear. At first Connor was concentrating so much on his footing and keeping an eye on P.J.'s progress that he didn't even notice the scenery around him.

Neil seemed to be interested in nothing but leading the way, and P.J. was doing fine, so Connor relaxed his vigilance. When they paused at a scenic point to take a rest, Connor sat down to drink in the beauty of the wild mountain scenery.

The area was beautiful in summer, but there was something wonderful and majestic about the craggy Rocky Mountains wearing their mantle of gray winter clothing. High above, pristine white snow glittered and flashed, reflecting the sun's brilliance. The sky was a deep shade of blue, and though the grass was brown and withered, it wasn't depressing, merely a sign that all was as it should be, that nature's cycle continued unabated despite their petty concerns, and would continue to do so for thousands of years yet to come. It was a bit humbling.

Connor almost felt in charity with Neil for bringing them here. The producer urged them to their feet, and they continued their trek. The going wasn't too bad, though the trip was uphill most of the way. Connor could see P.J. was starting to tire, though she wouldn't admit it, and he was glad when they finally spotted the wooden cabin.

Neil unlocked the door and led them into the cold mountain hut. Connor glanced around. The surroundings weren't as primitive as he'd feared. The wooden floor was made of planks, and the walls were rough-hewn timber. There were even two indoor bathrooms. He shared a relieved glance with P.J. It wasn't bad at all.

Neil knelt down to peer into the black cast-iron stove. "Looks like we'll need some more wood to last the night. There's plenty outside." He glanced at Connor. "You want to bring some in?"

Connor shrugged. "Sure." He went outside to get the wood and plotted his next move. He had to get close enough to Neil to touch the man's hand with his talisman—it was the only way he was going to find out for sure if he was the thief.

If he was, Connor would have all the evidence he'd need to convict the man and, as king of the Fae, he had the right to pass judgment and sentence immediately. If Neil wasn't guilty, they'd enjoy a day or two out here in the wilds of nature, then go home and start their investigation all over again from scratch.

As the sun began to dip beneath the horizon, Connor filled his arms with wood and went back inside. Neil had turned on the generator, and P.J. watched as Neil built a fire in the stove.

Good, if the room heated up, Neil would have no reason to wear those damned gloves and he'd have to take them off. Gradually the room warmed and Connor shed his jacket, motioning for P.J. to do the same. He glanced at Neil. "Neil, aren't you hot, man?"

Neil clapped his glove-clad hands together, then stuck them under his armpits. "No, I'm still a bit cold."

Apparently catching his train of thought, P.J. jumped into the fray. "Well, some good hot food will help that. And I, for one, am hungry. What's for dinner?"

Neil knelt down to rummage in his backpack. "Sorry it's nothing fancy, just trail rations, but I've got some stew and bread here—there are pots in the kitchen. Shall we get dinner started?"

P.J. leaned down to peer at the packages Neil had laid on the table. "Sure. I've never seen this type before—can I watch?"

Connor grinned inwardly. P.J. was making Neil live up to his promise to compensate for his earlier rudeness. She wasn't about to offer to play the little homemaker, and it appeared she was just as interested as Connor in how Neil was going to open those finicky little packages and cook them without taking off his gloves.

Neil looked distinctly taken aback. "I, uh, well...it's quite easy and the directions are on the package. Don't you think..." His voice trailed off as he apparently saw the stubborn lift of P.J.'s chin. "It's not rocket science, you know. Why don't you two...unpack and I'll start dinner."

How very big of him. "Does it matter where we sleep?" Connor asked.

Neil waved vaguely toward the bedrooms. "No, take any one, or two, you'd like."

"One," P.J. said in a decisive tone, and took Connor's arm.

Connor followed as she chose a large bedroom with a single bed and dumped her backpack down on the bed.

Connor lowered his voice. "Do you think 'tis wise, lass?"

P.J. grimaced. "How many times are you going to ask me that today? Yes, I think it's wise. If I have to sleep in the same house with Neil Chalmers, I want to make sure you're nearby."

She shrugged and lowered her gaze. "Besides, we may not have all that much time together, and I want to spend as much with you as possible," she muttered, refusing to meet his eyes.

Connor's pulse raced in spite of himself. She knew the score, yet she still wanted to be near him. He should be noble and offer to set protective spells around a separate room for her, but damned if he could pass up the opportunity to spend a little more time with her.

He tipped her chin up with one finger. "All right, lass, it'll be as you wish."

P.J. nodded and blushed, then said briskly, "Don't you know if Neil is the thief yet?"

"Uh, no. When I shook his hand, I thought there was something there. I can't explain it, but 'twas as if there was something blocking my senses, makin' it difficult for me to tell if he was the one or no. If I could just make him take off his gloves and touch his hand, I'd be able to tell in an instant."

P.J. nodded. "I thought it was something like that. Well, now that I know, maybe I can help you plan a way to trick him."

She finished unpacking her backpack, then stood on tiptoe and lifted her face shyly to his, twining her arms around his neck. "In the meantime, let's make the most of the time we have left."

She was so appealing, so trusting, Connor couldn't help but react. Tentatively at first, he lowered his head in an exploratory kiss that rediscovered the sweetness of her uninhibited response.

He deepened the kiss and she pressed herself tighter against him, making a small sound in the back of her throat that was Connor's undoing. P.J. was so open in her affections, so uncalculated and honest, it unmanned him. She had the rare gift of making him feel as if he were the only man in the universe, that she existed just to please him and to be pleased by him.

Connor's arms tightened around her as he buried his hands in her long dark hair and slanted a hungry kiss across her mouth.

A sound from the doorway caught his attention, and he lifted desire-blurred eyes to see Neil standing there, clearing his throat to get their attention.

Connor almost growled at him to get lost, until he noticed the man had removed his coat and gloves and was standing there with nothing more in his hands than a metal serving spoon.

Neil averted his gaze. "Uh, I just wanted to tell you dinner's ready," he said, then walked back to the kitchen.

Connor adjusted the fit of his suddenly snug pants. "If it weren't for the fact that he's shed those blasted gloves," he growled, "I'd tell him where he could put his dinner."

P.J. just smiled and kissed him. "That's okay, we've got all night. For now, it's important we unmask your thief."

"All right, but him bein' so close makes me nervous. Would you mind if I placed a bit of a warding spell on the room, so he can't overhear our conversations or enter without our permission?"

"Sounds like a good idea to me."

Connor quickly placed the spell, then followed P.J. to the dining room. He watched for an opportunity to touch Neil's hand, then suddenly realized the spoon Neil held was made of steel. Damn! The iron in steel would block any traces of magic.

Connor glanced around. Hell, all of the dishes and utensils were made of the same metal. Glowering, Connor watched Neil closely, waiting for him to let go of the spoon, if only for an instant. The man was too cagy, though. Once he finished dishing up the stew, he smoothly put down the spoon and picked up his fork in the same movement.

Seemingly oblivious of Connor's scrutiny, Neil turned to P.J. "Can I ask you some questions?" At P.J.'s apprehensive look, he said, "Don't worry, I won't pressure you to be my elf queen—I know you don't want that. But the story line has a great deal of magic in it and your sister told me you know a lot about it."

P.J. shrugged. "Sure, what kind of magic?"

"Well, in the film, the hero fights against the combined might of the evil elfin kingdom. The elves have magic and our hero doesn't, though he does possess a magic...amulet."

Connor had been only half listening, but now he sat up straighter. Was Neil asking what Connor thought he was asking?

Neil continued. "He knows it's magic, but he doesn't know how to use it. The book your sister sold me explained how to create a magic talisman, but not how to figure out what one does. How would he go about learning that, do you think?"

P.J. frowned, as if considering. "Well, according to talismanic lore, the physical appearance of the amulet often reveals its nature. What does it look like?"

Neil waved his fork in the air dismissively. "Oh, I haven't figured that out yet. Let's say it's a...a belt buckle."

"Okay, then I'd say the magic could be tied to the nature of a belt or a belt buckle. Since it's an article of clothing, maybe it simulates clothing, or makes the wearer invisible, or maybe it's a concealed weapon of some kind. It could be just about anything."

Neil leaned forward. "Okay, let's say it makes the hero invisible. Now, what if he doesn't know this? How would he find out?"

"Well, the best thing to do would be to ask the original owner or creator what its function is."

Connor almost chuckled out loud. In a way, that's exactly what Neil was doing. Did he really believe he wasn't a suspect? Apparently not, or he wouldn't be asking these questions.

"Okay," Neil conceded. "That makes sense. But we can't make things too easy on our hero. Let's say the person who made the amulet is dead. How would he go about finding out what it was used for and how to make it work?"

P.J. considered for a minute, and Connor interrupted, deciding to have a little fun with Neil. "Well, there's always the Killarney Ritual."

P.J. glanced askance at him, but apparently decided to play along. "Yes, I guess that would be the best way to find out."

Neil's nose seemed to quiver like a hound after a scent. "Oh, what's the Killarney Ritual? Is it something I could use in the film?"

Connor shrugged. "Sure, it can be used by anyone. The ritual is done at midnight, beneath the light of a full moon. Your hero will need to petition the gods outside, below the free and open sky, then draw a circle on the ground." There was a full moon tonight. Would Neil fall for it?

"Then what?" Neil asked eagerly.

"Next, he steps carefully into the circle, being careful not to smudge the line, and places the talisman between his upraised palms. Standing only upon his right foot, he sings to the gods—"

"Sings?" Neil queried. "Sings what?"

Connor shrugged. "It doesn't really matter what he sings, so long as the song has something to do with the amulet." Connor scratched his chin, thinking. "I'll not be knowin' any songs about belt buckles, so he'll have to make one up, I suppose."

Neil looked doubtful, so Connor groped for a way to make it more plausible. "Singing somehow... unlocks the potential of your mind, opening it up to receive divine revelation." When Neil nodded in understanding, Connor continued. "You have to do this three nights running, then on the third night you press the amulet to your forehead, and if the gods are pleased with your song, knowledge of the amulet's powers and how to use them will be given to you."

Neil nodded, frowning down into the steel cup clenched between his hands.

Connor risked a glance at P.J. and saw her trying hard to keep a straight face. "You forgot the most important part," she said.

"I did?"

"Yes, you forgot to mention that the supplicant must remove all of his clothes."

Connor smacked his forehead. "Ah, that's right. He mustn't have anything man-made on or about him, especially anything made of iron, or 'twill distract the gods. The only thing man-made he can have within the circle is the amulet." He gave Neil an innocent, earnest look. "Will that help?"

"Yes, I think I can work it in. Uh, this iron thing. I know iron interferes with the use of magic—does it work against all magic?"

"Yes, of course."

"Let's say my hero has a sword, then. Would that interfere with his finding out how the amulet works?"

"Most definitely. He'd have to take his sword off for the ritual to work."

"Not only that," P.J. interrupted. "But he'd have to leave it off for at least an hour—traces of the iron will linger for about that long and interfere with any magic he's working."

Neil's iron grip on the cup relaxed a bit, and Connor gave P.J. a grin for her quick thinking. It wasn't true, but if Neil thought it was, he might let go of that damned metal sometime soon.

Neil nodded. "You've given me a lot to think about. Thank you. I'm sure I'll be able to use this in the film." He yawned. "Now, if you'll excuse me, I think I'll go to bed. It's been a long day."

Connor returned his nod. "Sure, we'll be doing the same. See you in the morning."

Neil headed off to his bedroom, still clutching the damned cup in his hand. Once Neil had shut the door, Connor caught P.J. up in a big hug. "That was wonderful, you little pillywiggins."

P.J. giggled. "What on earth is a pillywiggins?"

"A flower faerie—a playful little thing just like you. What on earth made you think of telling him to dance naked?" he whispered softly.

P.J. shrugged. "I almost told him he'd have to paint himself blue, but I thought that would be going too far."

Connor stifled a guffaw and P.J. punched him softly. "Who was it who thought of the Killarney Ritual, anyway? Blarney Ritual is more like it. Besides, I saw you looking frustrated, so I thought I'd give you an edge, and give him a good reason to let go of his iron security blanket."

"Aye, that you did," Connor said, smiling down at her. "Now let's hope he fell for it."

P.J. nodded, then wriggled loose from his embrace. "I want to check something." She walked over to the corner where Neil had laid his gloves on the table and picked one up. "Let's see...." She stuck her hand in it, then grinned and turned the palm inside out. "It seems Neil already knew a bit about iron. Look, he has a steel plate in the palm of his glove."

"So that's why his grip felt so hard and why I couldn't feel any traces of magic."

"You know what that means, don't you?" P.J. whispered.

"What?"

"This means he must be the thief! Why else would he be wearing a steel plate in his glove?"

Connor nodded slowly. "Aye, 'twould appear that way. But I'll not be jumpin' to conclusions anymore. I must touch his hand and get the evidence firsthand."

He took the glove and put it back on the table. "Come, let's go to bed and see if we can come up with a plan."

P.J. took a shower first, and returned to the bedroom while Connor washed the grime of the hike off his body. Feeling clean once more, he slipped his briefs back on and made his way back to the bedroom. The bedroom lights were turned off and Connor had trouble seeing at first. He could tell she'd laid out the bedrolls, but couldn't quite make out if P.J. was in them or not. Was she asleep?

He turned quietly to place his clothes on a chair and inhaled sharply.

P.J.'s perfect lithe figure, bare of all clothing, was outlined by the light of the full moon. She stood in front of the window, her face partly in shadow as she turned toward him. The dappled moonlight filtering through the trees made mysterious shadows across her body, figleafing the triangle below her belly and hiding one perfect breast from view.

Connor shamelessly drank in her beauty and perfection as she stood still for his perusal. God, she was so beautiful it hurt. His briefs became unbearably tight and he eased the waistband away from his body. P.J.'s gaze flickered downward and Connor groaned. His desire was evident—there was no sense in hiding it. "Oh, lass," he breathed.

"I know I said I wouldn't, but just one last time...?"

The husky timbre of her voice vibrated through him, eliciting a thrumming response. He knew what she wanted, and he had no power to refuse her.

He crossed the room in two swift steps and came to a halt in front of her, gazing down at the smoky desire reflected in her eyes. Pulling her into his arms, he molded her soft body against his. The night air had cooled her skin, making her nipples pebble hard against his chest. He ran his hands over the soft curves of her back and buttocks, warming her with his heat.

"Oh, God, you feel so good," he murmured into the clean, crisp mountain scent of her hair.

P.J.'s body warmed and her arms tightened around him. "So do you, but it's cold out here!" She released him for a moment and tugged him toward the waiting bed.

Connor followed her willingly, and he quickly shucked his briefs, then scrambled into the sleeping bag beside her. They shivered together for a few moments before their body heat merged, creating a warm oasis beneath the covers. Connor pulled them up over his head so they wouldn't lose one iota of this precious heat and snuggled into her warmth.

He avidly captured her lips, a tide of longing rising within him at her uninhibited response. Their lips touched, parted, then touched again as they explored the wonder of each other. His tongue dipped into the sweetness of her mouth and she moaned, drawing him inside in a sudden savage suction that sent waves of desire coursing through his body to center in his throbbing erection. He groaned and pressed himself against her.

But first, before he could find sweet relief, he had to take care of P.J. He stilled her hands between his large ones, and with long, wet kisses and slow caresses of his mouth and tongue, he pleasured her, bringing her to the pinnacle not once, but twice.

Finally, she protested that she couldn't take any more, and returned the favor, using her mouth and gentle fingers so skillfully he was ready to explode within seconds. She continued her sweet torture until he finally tore her hands away. "Now," he pleaded harshly.

"Yes, now." She ceased her ministrations and rolled over to retrieve a small packet from the bedside table, helping him sheathe himself in its contents. "But we do it my way." She sat astride him, then slowly eased down over him, until he filled her completely.

Her throbbing warmth was too much. He plunged urgently ~~within~~ her, grasping her hips as if they were a lifeline. She met him thrust for thrust and the powerful exhilaration mounted, rolling over him in waves until the universe exploded around him in a million shards of glittering stardust. His cries joined hers as she, too, climaxed once more and pulsed around him, then relaxed to lie spent and unmoving on his chest.

P.J. kissed his damp chest and sighed. "Was it as good for you as it was for me?"

Connor chuckled at her imitation of his voice as she repeated the question he'd asked in the tiny car days ago. "Aye," he whispered. "Better."

She rolled off his chest and curled up next to him. "Were we loud? Do you think Neil heard us?"

"No, the wards ensure he can't—" Connor broke off, hearing something outside. "Shh, what's that noise?"

They stilled, and gradually a man's voice off in the distance became clear, soaring through the night air, singing, "...knick-knack, paddy-whack, give the dog a bone..."

Connor and P.J. exploded into laughter, muffling it beneath the covers.

"Oh, no," gasped P.J. "Can't you just see it—Neil standing in a circle on one foot—"

"All naked and shriveled up in the cold—"

"Singing about a *shoehorn!*"

Connor's chuckles finally died and he said, "Lord, I wish I could see this. I wonder what verse he changed to fit in the shoehorn."

P.J.'s paroxysms of laughter devolved to mere giggles. "I don't know, but this pretty much proves he's got the thing, wouldn't you say?"

"Aye, and 'twould serve him right if he caught his death of cold. I still need incontrovertible proof, though. I've got to touch his hand. Will you help me, lass?"

"Of course. What do you want me to do?"

"Well, 'tis only me Neil seems to be avoidin'. He doesn't seem to have a problem touching you at all. Now, my ring will work just as well if you're holding it. If you were to take it and wait until he lets go of the iron—"

P.J. shook her head. "No, I'm afraid my allergy to gold will get in the way. If I hold the ring too long, the itching will make me crazy and he'd suspect something. No, it's better if we just wait for a good opportunity and nail him. Between the two of us, he doesn't stand a chance."

That almost-memory nagged at him again—something to do with allergies. Unable to pin it down, Connor shrugged and gave it up for the moment. "All right, but if we don't do this soon, I'll have to sit on the man and beat him until he lets go of the iron."

P.J. nodded back. "And I'll help. But for now, let's get some sleep."

Chapter Twelve

The next morning Connor woke to find P.J. gone from the bed. When her missing status slowly pierced his foggy brain, he sat up with a start. Dear God, what if Neil had done something to her?

Connor leapt out of bed, pausing only to pull on his shorts. His heart pounding, he thundered into the main cabin, only to find P.J. standing calmly next to Neil where he was stirring some eggs on the stove with a metal spatula.

They both turned to look at Connor with their mouths round in astonishment. A cool breeze feathered over his body, and he realized how foolish he looked. He gaped at the two of them, trying to find something, anything, to say.

"Connor!" P.J. screeched. "Put some clothes on. You'll catch your death of cold!"

She grabbed the spatula out of Neil's hands and shoved him toward Connor. "Help him find a robe, something," she said in a shrill tone that wasn't a bit like her.

As Connor stood rooted in embarrassment, Neil took a tentative step toward him.

"Hurry up," P.J. said, and shoved Neil a little harder, somehow managing to trip him at the same time.

Neil hit the floor face first at Connor's bare feet. Seizing the opportunity thus afforded, Connor steeled himself to show no reaction no matter what Neil's hands revealed, and grabbed the man to help him up.

Once Connor's ring touched him, the tingling was almost like an electric shock. Yes, Neil had handled Stayle's talisman—and very recently too. At long last they'd found their thief.

Well? P.J. demanded silently as she held her breath and watched Connor closely, waiting for his verdict. A flash of triumph appeared in his eyes, though he quickly suppressed it. Yes! They'd found their thief.

Connor admirably suppressed what had to be an urgent desire to demand the shoehorn back immediately, and suddenly seemed to remember his lack of clothing. P.J. didn't mind it, but it was rude of them to display Connor's magnificence before the puny Neil.

With a muttered excuse, Connor slipped off to the bedroom to finish dressing. P.J. thrust the spatula into Neil's hand with a hasty apology and followed Connor into the bedroom.

As Connor slipped on his shirt, P.J. bounded over to whisper in his ear. "You got your proof, didn't you?"

He flashed her a grim smile and slipped on his shoes. "Aye, lass, that I did. His hands made my ring tingle like 'twas afire." He leaned down to give her a swift, sweet kiss. "And thank you for thinkin' so quickly—he's the thief, all right."

"That's wonderful! Why don't we just grab the shoehorn and go?"

"'Tisn't that simple, lass. For one thing, we don't know where 'tis. And he's had it a good long time now and has handled it a lot. The talisman is tryin' to key itself to its new owner and will resist detection by magic. The best thing to do now is to find out where it is so I can take it away by physical means."

P.J. was a little disappointed it wasn't going to be as easy as she'd thought, but she was game for anything. "Okay, now what do we do?"

"*We* don't do anything," he said as he tucked his shirt into the waistband of his jeans. "You leave, and I'll get my sister's talisman back."

"Leave? Hell, no, I'm not gonna leave," she whispered fiercely.

Connor looked up from tying his shoes. "It could be dangerous now, lass. I'm going to have to wrest the talisman away from him physically, and I don't want you in the way when it happens."

He rose and took her in his arms, kissing her lightly on the nose. "You're too precious to risk in a confrontation like this."

"But our bargain—I agreed to help you find the talisman in exchange for the custom-made shoes and my story. I have to see it through or the bargain is null and void."

P.J. knew her argument was weak, but maybe it would penetrate Connor's ridiculously old-fashioned attitude and appeal to his sense of fair play.

He kissed her again, this time on the forehead. "Nice try, lass, but after everything you've done to help me, our bargain is complete. If it weren't for you

and your quick thinking, I'd still be wonderin' if Neil
was really the one. Now I know." He gazed at her se-
riously, relentlessly. "And 'tis time for you to go, out
of danger. You promised."

"What about you? Isn't it dangerous for you, too?"

"Nay, I've magic to protect me, y'know. And
'twould be best if I don't have the worry about shield-
in' you along with it. Without your full name, I can't
protect you as I'd wish."

P.J. bit her lip. Her curiosity demanded she stay for
the denouement. She could, *if* she gave Connor her
true name now.

Suddenly, with a blinding flash of insight, she realized she did trust him. Connor was so good and de-
cent and honest, she knew she could trust him with all
of her innermost secrets—even her name. No matter
what happened, she knew he would never betray her
trust. He couldn't, and still be the man she had grown
to love. The knowledge filled her with a wild exulta-
tion.

She opened her mouth to share her discovery, but
stopped when she realized how it would look to him.
If she told him her name now, he'd think it was only
because she wanted to satisfy her vulgar curiosity. No,
she couldn't do that and risk losing his trust and respect.

She tried another tack. "But the weather outside is
awful." She pointed at the window. "See, it snowed
last night, despite the predictions. How am I going to
leave?"

Connor frowned. "Don't worry about that. I'll
magic you up some skis, then."

"But I can't ski," she said triumphantly.

"You've lived in Vail all your life and you can't ski?"

"No, I never learned. It always seemed like such a desecration of nature's beauty, and the skiers are so obsessed with speed and exhilaration, I never wanted to learn. Really," she exclaimed when he looked doubtful.

He nodded. "All right, then, I'll get you some snowshoes."

She opened her mouth to protest, but he got there first. "Damn it, woman, I don't care if you're allergic to snowshoes and they give you the green willies, you're going to leave! I'll find some way to get you down off this mountain, and that's that."

P.J.'s mouth firmed in a straight line. Like hell he was. She was determined to see this through to the bitter end.

He smoothed a strand of hair back from her face. "Don't you see, lass? You're too precious to risk, and I must do this myself. My sister, my people, are counting on me."

His simple words struck home. She'd forgotten that his position hinged on his successful completion of this mission, not to mention his sister's sanity. How would he feel if he went back to his people and told them that she—a mere mortal—had solved the riddle for him and captured the crook? He'd be a laughingstock, and it would all be P.J.'s fault.

Unfortunately he'd just found the one argument that would sway her. "All right," she said. "When should I leave?"

She felt Connor's body relax. She hadn't realized how tense he'd been up to now, and was rather touched at this sign of his concern.

He captured her lips in a gentle kiss. "Right after breakfast. We'll pretend to go for a walk, then you head down to the car. After I'm sure you're far enough away, I'll tell Neil we had a fight and you left. All right, lass?"

P.J. agreed. She wasn't looking forward to making that three-mile trek back to the car alone, but she guessed she owed it to Connor. How ironic—if only she'd told him her name last night, she could've saved herself the trip.

A sudden thought struck her. "The car—it's Neil's and I don't have the keys. What am I supposed to do, walk all the way back to Vail? Or worse yet, hitch-hike?"

Connor frowned. "No, I saw Neil put them in his coat pocket. I'll distract him, and you get the keys."

P.J. nodded. "Okay, but how are you going to get back if I take the car?"

"Magic, of cour—"

He broke off as they heard a knock on the door. Neil's voice came through muffled. "Breakfast is ready. Are you coming?"

Connor sighed and raised his voice. "Aye, we're comin'. We'll be there in just a moment."

He gave P.J. another kiss and released her from his warmth, then they joined Neil at the dining-room table. He'd dished up a wonderful-smelling breakfast of eggs, sausage and toast. Neil sneezed and P.J. stifled a grin. He didn't seem to be feeling too well—it appeared his nocturnal ritual had given the man a head cold. Well, P.J. felt no sympathy—not even a twinge. It served him right.

They finished the meal and Neil stood, gathering the dishes together. "So, what shall we do today? We can—"

Connor interrupted him gently. "You promised us a quiet weekend away from the hustle and bustle. We'd like a little time to be alone. Isn't that right, lass?"

P.J. nodded. "Yes, if you don't mind, Neil. We'd like to take a nice walk together. We have something we need to...work out." She might as well start setting up her angry departure now to make it more believable.

"But—" Neil protested.

"Wait, let me explain," Connor said, and drew Neil aside, casting a significant glance back over his shoulder to where their coats hung by the door.

P.J. didn't need him to draw her a picture. She crossed to the door, and while Connor spoke in low, urgent tones to Neil, keeping the producer's back to her, she fished the keys out of the first pocket she looked in. Giving Connor a thumbs-up, she shoved them in her own coat pocket and shrugged into her coat. "Connor," she exclaimed querulously. "Come on, let's go."

Connor rolled his eyes for Neil's benefit, then finished his low-voiced conversation. "All right, lass, I'm comin'."

They managed to escape from the cabin with very little ado, and took off on a path that not so coincidentally led down toward the car. Once they were out of sight of the hut, P.J. glanced down the snow-covered path with trepidation. She'd agreed to leave, but it didn't look like it would be easy, especially since the air seemed to be about twenty degrees cooler than the day before.

Connor must've caught her apprehension, for he said, "No second thoughts now, lass."

"No, it's just that I'm not sure I can find the path down. It's not real easy to see beneath the snow."

Connor nodded slowly. "You're right." He pulled her collar tighter up around her neck. "But I'm going to give you all the advantages I possibly can. You deserve it for being such a good sport." He kissed her on the nose. "And I want to make sure nothing happens to you, either."

P.J. felt all warm inside, as if he'd just filled her with a magic heat. Right now she'd do anything he wanted—anything to keep him looking at her like that. "But how can you justify expending all that magic? What about your promise?"

"That doesn't apply when someone's safety is in jeopardy—faerie or mortal. Not even the Fae would expect me to ignore the need of someone in danger."

Some of her elation faded. He'd do the same for anyone, of course. She was silly to read any more into it.

Connor released her and took off his gloves. Touching his talisman ring, he frowned down at the ground. Slowly, an emerald green sheen came over the snow, then curved into a two-foot-wide path that stretched down the length of the trail.

Connor sighed. "There. Just follow the green and it'll lead you down to the car."

"Aren't you taking a risk that someone will see it?"

"Perhaps, but since Neil booked the entire cabin, there shouldn't be too many people up here, anyway. And, just to make sure, the green will disappear behind you."

Clever. It would also keep P.J. from returning the same way.

Connor touched his ring once more and concentrated. P.J. felt her clothing warm up—even her hat and shoes. She looked at him in surprise.

Connor grinned. "That ought to keep you warm for your trip down the mountain—and I put an avoidance spell on you so the animals won't bother you. But just in case, I'll give you something of mine to use as a locator." He fished in his pockets and came out with a comb. "Well, 'tis better than nothing." He concentrated again. "Here, take this. Put it somewhere where you can get to it quickly. If you get into trouble, just hold on tight and call my name. I'll be there instantly."

P.J. took the proffered comb and carefully put it in the jacket pocket opposite of Neil's keys so the metal in them wouldn't negate the magic. "Okay, but forget the snowshoes. I don't know how to use them and the snow's not all that deep, anyway. I'm sure my boots can handle it."

She hugged him, putting all her pent-up feelings—relief, caring, sorrow at their parting—into that simple gesture. She was reluctant to let go.

Connor finally pried her arms loose. "You'll be all right, lass, you'll see. And I'll be seein' you again, if you'll let me."

P.J.'s heart soared with relief. That had been her only remaining worry, but no more. Connor was as good as his word. If he said he'd see her again, he meant just that. She gave him a long, hard passionate kiss to remind him of the night they'd shared together, and released him reluctantly.

"You'd best be going now," he said.

"All right, but you be careful." Connor had thought of everything, and she was sure she could make it down to the car safe and sound.

"I will," he promised. "I'll just watch until your trail disappears, then I'll go back to the cabin and confront Neil. Don't worry, everything will be fine. With any luck I'll be able to find the talisman right away, send Neil off to jail and join you on the path." He touched the pocket where she'd tucked the comb. "This'll help me find you."

P.J. sighed and started the long trek down the hill. She might as well hurry up and get it over with. Her spirits lifted as she realized the sooner she got out of sight, the sooner Connor could get the shoehorn and join her.

The going was a lot easier than she'd expected, and soon she started moving faster, with more confidence. It was actually kind of nice, being out here in the midst of nature all alone, knowing she was in no danger and couldn't get lost.

If only Connor were here, it would be perfect. She smiled ruefully. Just a week ago she would've scoffed at the idea that he could protect her magically, and now she was accepting it like it was a natural part of her life. It wasn't difficult, when the evidence was so clear all around her: the green path, the heated clothing, which seemed to cool as her body generated its own heat, and the—

"Oof!" She tripped over a rock hidden in the snow and twisted, landing on her side. "Damn!" Unfortunately the magic didn't protect her from her own stupidity. If she'd been watching the path instead of daydreaming about Connor, she would've seen the damned rock and wouldn't have tripped.

Oh well, she'd live. Only her pride was hurt. She glanced back up the path. The hut was long since out of sight, so Connor hadn't seen her ignominious fall from grace. P.J. stumbled to her feet and brushed the snow off, then continued walking, watching her steps more carefully this time.

Two hours later she finally reached the end of the trail and found Neil's snow-covered car still waiting at the bottom. There was no sense waiting for Connor. He could join her wherever she was, and Neil didn't deserve to find his car.

P.J. patted her jacket pocket, relieved to find the keys still there. She hadn't thought to check for them when she'd fallen, and thank goodness she wasn't paying the price for her inattention.

She started the car and turned the defrosters on, then popped the trunk to see if Neil had an ice scraper. She rummaged around in the cluttered trunk and finally spotted a length of flat red plastic sticking out from under a tarp toward the rear. That had to be it. She grasped the tarp and pulled, then stared in surprise at what she had revealed.

A ruby-and-diamond bracelet winked and sparkled in the sunlight, next to a silk scarf, a pair of expensive leather gloves, a silver pen—

Wait, was that...? P.J. picked up the pen and examined it. Sure enough, it had her initials on it. This was *her* pen. So that's where it had disappeared to. But how had Neil . . . ?

She glanced down at the stash where her pen had been hiding. Amaranth's crystal snowflake was there, too. She froze, stunned as the truth struck her. Neil had stolen it, just as he had stolen all of this other stuff.

But why? He was a rich, successful producer. What did he need with a woman's scarf, or a stolen bracelet, or a monogrammed pen, for heaven's sake?

Kleptomania—that had to be it. P.J. tried to recall what she knew about the condition. From what she remembered, kleptomania caused the sufferer to steal. The usefulness or cost of the item was irrelevant, it was the stealing that was important.

So that's why he'd stolen the shoehorn—up until now, P.J. had been at a loss to discern his motive. She glanced back at the loot in the trunk. Well, now that she knew, what should she do about it? Try to return it to the real owners? But how would she find them?

The winking diamonds caught her eye and she was suddenly struck by the memory of the woman at the hotel who'd complained of her bracelet being stolen. Aha! That string of thefts that had followed them around was now finally explained—Neil was the culprit. She searched her memory. What else had come up missing? There was the pen, the bracelet—

Oh, no. The gun.

Quickly she searched the rest of the trunk, tossing things aside in her haste. Everything else was here. Where was the damned gun? She suddenly felt nauseous—Neil had to have it with him.

She froze. Connor was waiting up there and about to confront Neil, not knowing the man carried a pistol.

Sudden realization made her relax. What was she worried about? Connor's magic would protect him. She grinned, imagining what Neil's reaction would be to Connor's nonchalance as he pointed the cold steel—

Steel! Dear God, guns and bullets had iron in them. What could she do? That was the one thing Connor's magic couldn't protect him from. She had to do something to help him, warn him. But what?

The comb!

All she had to do was pull out the comb and call Connor. He could just pop back to the hut the same way he'd pop here, but this time he'd be forewarned. She stuck her hand in her pocket to pull out the comb.

It wasn't there.

She searched deeper. Still no comb.

Maybe her other pocket? Frantically she searched all her pockets, to no avail. Where was the damned thing?

Her fingers stilled as she remembered her fall. She'd fallen on the same side where she'd put the comb. Hell, that's where it was—two-thirds of the way up the trail.

She slumped in despair. Now what was she going to do? Her only hope of warning Connor was two miles up the mountain and she was here at the bottom. She couldn't even follow the trail back up, because the magic had disappeared.

She glanced at the snow-covered path in despair and straightened, her hopes rising. Well, the green was gone, but her footsteps were clearly visible in the snow.

She could follow them to the top and warn him herself.

P.J. nodded decisively. She wasn't looking forward to the trek back up the mountain, but how else could she warn Connor? It should be easy to find the comb—the snow was bound to be a lot more trampled where she'd fallen.

Then again, her fall hadn't been too far from the cabin. She could just as easily hike all the way back to the hut and save as much of Connor's magic as possible. Yes, that was much better.

Resolutely, P.J. turned off the engine and locked the car, turning back to the path before her.

Chapter Thirteen

Connor watched until P.J. was out of sight and sighed in relief when he could no longer see the magical path. Now he could concentrate on Neil without having to worry about protecting her. Just to ensure she was safe, he gave her enough time to make it all the way to the bottom of the mountain before he put his plan into effect.

Devising a plan to persuade Neil to reveal the location of the shoehorn hadn't been easy—the best he could come up with was the old pretend-to-be-drunk trick. If Neil thought Connor was soused, the thieving bastard might relax his vigilance long enough for Connor to learn something.

Connor nodded decisively and conjured up a bottle of Chivas to make his story more authentic. No, on second thought, that would be pushing belief too much. Regretfully he consigned the Chivas to oblivion and called up a quart bottle of a less expensive brand. He splashed about a third of its contents on his clothing, then took a swig and converted the alcohol to water in his stomach. Time to put on his own one-man show.

Connor made his way to the cabin and opened the door, then slammed it shut. Pulling his jacket off, he dumped it on the floor, then staggered in drunkenly. Neil looked up from where he was reading a book at the table—the same book Amaranth had just sold him—and grabbed a metal cup.

Good, his audience was in place. Connor crossed the room to join Neil, banged the whiskey down on the table and slumped into a chair. "Damn woman," he muttered, just loud enough for Neil to hear.

Neil's eyes widened as he took the bait. He glanced back at the closed door. "Where's P.J.? What happened?"

"Ah, nothin'." Connor intentionally slurred his words. "We jus' had a little fight, thas all." Would a hiccup be too much? Probably. He squelched the urge to overact.

Connor squinted up at Neil. "She gave me hell about my comin' out almost starkers this mornin'. Hell, 'tisn't as if you were a woman. I don't know what her problem is." He took another swallow.

Neil's face contorted in mock sympathy. "Yes, women can be the very devil. Where is she now?"

Connor waved the bottle grandly. "Took off. Said she wasn't going to stick around and watch me make a macho fool of myself. Me, a macho fool? Ha! Said she'd walk all the way back to town or hitchhike if she had to." Connor took another swallow as Neil appeared to digest that information.

"Wan' some?" Connor offered the bottle. It wouldn't hurt to get Neil a little drunk, either.

"No, thanks—"

Ignoring Neil's protest, Connor grabbed a metal cup and filled it with whiskey. With the trouble those cups had given him, they might as well be good for something. "C'mon—join me, thas a pal. Man should never drink alone, y'know." He tipped some into the cup Neil was clutching.

Neil took a sip. "Not bad. Where'd you get it?"

"Found it stuck in a hole. Damn near tripped over the blasted thing." He blinked at the bottle. "P.J. didn't like that, either. Hell, she knows I don't drink. At least not usually." He leaned over and added in a confiding tone, "I don' hold my liquor well, y'see. But there's no call for her to be so nasty about it."

Neil's eyes gleamed as he raised his cup to Connor. "Well, to hell with her and all women!"

"Amen!" Connor said, and downed the contents of his cup. Now, how to get Neil onto the right subject?

He glanced down at the book Neil was reading. "Thas a pretty good book," he said. "But it leaves a lot out, y'know."

Neil perked up at that. "Oh, like what?"

Connor shrugged. "Lots of things." He busied himself by peering with what he hoped was a brooding look into the depths of the shallow cup, inwardly chafing at Neil's slowness in taking the bait.

"Can you be more specific?" Neil asked.

"Depends on what you'll be wantin' to know." Connor laid a finger against his nose. "There be lots of things we Irish know that we'll not be after tellin' the likes of some writer. We have our secrets, too, and we'll be keepin' 'em."

Neil poured Connor another cup of the whiskey and took a sip himself. Damn, the man wasn't drinking as much as Connor would've preferred. Surreptitiously, Connor concentrated on changing the whiskey in Neil's stomach to pure alcohol, but was balked by a wall of magic. Stayle's talisman must be close by, if it was protecting him this well. Connor upped the stakes.

"Ha! Most of what P.J. learned, she learned from me." He winked at Neil. "But I didn't tell her everything, y'know. After all, I'm the only one who can identify the thief when we find him. But it makes it really tough when she won't even tell me what we're looking—" He broke off suddenly, making it appear as if he'd said too much. "Ah, never mind."

"No, this is fascinating. I might be able to use it in my movie."

Connor almost grinned but schooled his voice to sound suitably indignant. "Here she is, with a hefty fee to find a missin' talisman, and she's sure she knows who the bleedin' thief is, and she won't even tell me what the talisman is!"

Neil's expression turned sly and crafty. "Who's the thief?"

"Oh, some Brit magician who won't even let us near him," Connor muttered.

Neil visibly relaxed. "So, you don't know what the talisman is?"

Good, he'd swallowed it, hook, line and sinker. "Nay, all I know is the client is a woman—it's probably some gewgaw or other."

Neil brightened. "Say, I've got a talisman I bought with the book. They told me it was magic, but I don't know what it does. Do you think you could tell me?"

Hooked! Now all he had to do was reel him in. Connor shrugged, continuing to play it cool. "Sure, 'tis easy enough, and I'll not be needing the Killarney Ritual, either. Thas only for magic-blind folk like her, y'know."

"Good, I'll get it." Neil rose and headed toward the door.

No, don't tell me... Connor had dismissed the jackets and packs as being too obvious, too easy. He cursed himself as Neil reached into an inside pocket of his jacket. If only P.J. hadn't found the keys in the first pocket she'd checked.

Connor fought to control a surge of elation as Neil pulled his hand out and Connor caught the glint of gold. The talisman! Continuing the sham, Connor stumbled to his feet. "Whas—"

He froze as a call resounded through his mind. *Connor!* P.J. called, using the magic comb he'd given her.

P.J. was in trouble! But now, with victory so near, what should he do? Try to wrestle the shoehorn away from Neil, or go to P.J.? He hesitated for only a moment. Neil would keep. P.J. came first.

But it wouldn't do to disappear in front of the man, who was even now beginning to look wary. Connor quickly changed his stumble into a stagger toward the bathroom. "I'll be right back," he muttered.

At least Neil wouldn't be suspicious. He'd never believe a man would take a detour to the bathroom when he had success so close at hand.

Connor closed the door and concentrated on teleporting himself to P.J., preparing himself to be ready for anything that might be threatening her. He concentrated on the comb in P.J.'s possession and poured all his power through the ring to transport himself instantly to her location.

He moved through space and found himself abruptly outside—in front of the cabin. *What the devil?*

P.J. appeared then, motioning to him from behind a tree. He joined her, exasperated. "What are you doin' here? I told you—"

"Shh," P.J. cautioned. "He'll hear you. I lost the comb when I fell on the trail and had to come back and find it."

He grasped her shoulders. "Why? What was so important that you had to risk your life?"

"Remember all those things that were stolen on the trip—my pen, the bracelet—"

"Aye, but what has that to do with this?"

"I found them in Neil's car—he's a kleptomaniac and he's been behind all the burglaries on our trip."

"All right, so now we know why he took the shoehorn. You came back to tell me this?"

"No, no, I came back to tell you he's also got the—" Her eyes widened as she stared openmouthed at something behind Connor.

He whirled around—too late. Neil whipped past him to grab P.J. and point a very lethal .38 at her temple. Connor froze.

Neil smiled nastily, saying, "He's also got the gun." His arm tightened across P.J.'s neck. "Isn't that what you were about to say?"

Connor could see the fear in P.J.'s eyes as she looked at him imploringly. Fear constricted his heart—he couldn't breathe. What could he do? How could he save her?

He aborted the instinct to call upon his magic. It had always been there for him, but now, the one time in his life he really needed it, he was helpless. Because of P.J.'s inability to trust him with her name, he was unable to use his only means of rescuing her.

Connor clenched his fists in frustration. He couldn't affect Neil magically, either, not when Neil had P.J., the gun and the shoehorn. How ironic. If only P.J. hadn't been there, he could've very easily protected himself—there were ways of avoiding iron even if he was vulnerable to it. But now...

Connor was stymied. Neil had won.

Neil must have seen the defeat in his eyes. "So you thought you could fool me, eh? Well, you're not as clever as you think. I saw the change in your eyes, and knew then you weren't drunk. I heard you talking and came out to find you plotting with this sweet little thing."

Neil waved the gun around as if he were the villain in a bad melodrama and sneered. "You were good, real good. You almost had me buying it, too, but I can spot a lousy actor a mile away."

Connor grimaced, and Neil laughed in triumph. "Besides, you forgot one little thing. I overheard you talking about the talisman in Melissa's condo that first day. You said then you'd be able to identify the man who stole the *shoehorn* if you could just touch his hand. You knew all along what the talisman was. You lied to me."

Neil sounded highly indignant, and it was all Connor could do to control the urge to laugh hysterically. The man had stolen Stayle's talisman, had cut a thieving swath across half of Europe and God knew where else, was holding P.J. hostage with a gun at her head and he was upset at Connor for telling a little fib!

Wisely, Connor chose not to point this out. He didn't dare antagonize the man further. Especially since the fear in P.J.'s eyes pulled at him, pleading with him to do something.

Neil smiled grimly. "Now let's go back inside where it's warmer, shall we?"

Connor nodded and walked slowly back into the hut, his fists clenching and unclenching as he fumed inwardly at his helplessness. Neil followed him closely, clutching P.J. as if she were his lifeline. She was. The moment Neil released P.J., he was history. Connor would make sure of that.

Neil kicked the door shut behind him and gestured with his gun toward an empty wall. "Stand over there where I can see you."

Connor did so and Neil smiled evilly. "Now, finally, tell me how to work this thing." He gestured with the shoehorn, pressing it cruelly, ludicrously, into P.J.'s white throat like a knife.

Connor played for a little time. "In order for you to key it properly, I have to know why you want to use it and what you plan to use it for."

Neil frowned and his grip on P.J. tightened noticeably. "If you're putting me on—"

Connor allowed genuine fear to enter his voice. "I'm not—really. This is an important part of keying the talisman to you. Tell him, P.J."

P.J. gamely nodded beneath Neil's grip. Connor's heart constricted. She must be terrified and desperate to be away, yet she still played his game like a trooper.

Neil's grip loosened and he nodded slowly. "All right, the book did say something about that. I didn't know what I had until you explained it so nicely at Melissa's. I realized then it was the very thing I needed."

Connor nodded, encouraging him to go on. He knew most crooks had a burning desire to explain their cleverness. If Connor could get Neil to talk about himself, maybe the man would relax enough to loosen his hold on the shoehorn.

"I know this film will be a blockbuster," Neil continued, "if only I can get backing. But it's too expensive because of the massive special effects involved." He shrugged, grinning. "So I figured if I could control real magic, I wouldn't need special effects—or backing."

Neil's grip relaxed for a moment and Connor tensed, prepared to spring when the chance presented itself. Unfortunately Neil recalled the situation and tightened his grip on P.J. "Okay, I told you. Now how do I key it?"

"First, let P.J. go."

"Oh, no. I'm not falling for that. Tell me first, and we'll test it, then I'll let her go."

Well, it had been worth a try, though Connor hadn't expected it to work. He sighed. Damn the shoehorn! The only thing that was important was P.J. No more games. "All right, the truth. You can't use it—you have to have magic of your own to be able to key it to yourself. It'll never work for you."

Neil's face was suffused with a red wash of anger. He pulled the hammer back on the gun and shoved it harder against P.J.'s temple. "I don't believe you. Now tell the truth."

Connor stood helplessly, not knowing what to do. How could he convince Neil he had told the truth?

Connor's gaze sought P.J.'s. Her eyes were filled with a resigned acknowledgment of her fate. She knew he wasn't lying and that her remaining life was measured in seconds. Connor froze in fear, not knowing what to do.

P.J. moistened her lips. "He is telling the truth," she assured Neil, her voice cracking with fear.

"Shut up," Neil growled, and turned impatiently back to Connor. It was obvious the man was on the edge and it wouldn't take much to push him over.

Connor glanced helplessly at P.J., wishing he could take her into his arms just once more. "I'm sorry, P.J.," he said, knowing it was totally inadequate to express how he felt.

Her heart showing in her tear-filled eyes, P.J. swallowed hard. Her mouth twisted in a wry smile. "It's not P.J.... it's Petunia. Petunia Jonquil."

Petunia Jonquil? The absurdity of her name, coupled with the stressful situation, bubbled up inside him, forcing out a semihysterical chuckle. He couldn't help it—he doubled over and howled with laughter.

The exasperation on his Petunia's face and the shock on Neil's only sent Connor into further paroxysms.

Luckily P.J. wasn't so helpless. Taking swift advantage of Neil's suddenly loosened grip, she knocked the shoehorn out of his hand. "Connor, here!" she yelled.

The shoehorn skittered across the floor to land at Connor's feet. He snatched it up and sobered quickly. Now that he was armored with the knowledge of P.J.'s name and Stayle's shoehorn, Neil was one dead thief.

P.J. jammed her elbow into Neil's stomach and ducked out of the way as Connor slammed Neil's gun hand against the wall and slugged him with all the pent-up force of his frustration. Disappointingly, Neil crumpled at the first blow.

Connor stood over him in frustrated rage, then with a wave of his hand he pronounced Neil's full name and sent him to a cold dark cell to await his fate.

Only then did he turn to P.J. and gather her into his arms. They clung to each other and he covered her upturned face with a dozen tiny kisses. "Dear God, I thought I'd lost you. Don't ever do that to me again!"

P.J. shuddered in his arms and nodded. "Never again, I promise." They just stood there, holding each other for a few more moments as they took a well-deserved breather. "I changed my mind," P.J. muttered. "I don't want to stay here after all. I just want to go home, but I'm so tired I don't think I'll be able to make it down that mountain again."

Connor kissed the top of her head. "That's not necessary now, now that I know your name... Petunia." Finally, when he'd thought all was lost, she'd trusted him with her true name. He'd never been given a better gift.

P.J. shot him a wary glance. "Forget you ever heard that, okay?"

Connor laughed and hugged her. "All right, lass."

Then, between one breath and the next, he transferred them and all their belongings to the workroom of Stayle's shop.

P.J. looked around in astonishment, but now Connor's eyes were all for his patient sister who had waited so long for her talisman.

Stayle jumped in alarm at their sudden appearance, but Connor merely held up the shoehorn. Stayle's eyes widened, and he could see the cares and sorrows of the past few weeks fall away like magic as she shrieked with joy and came charging across the room to grab the talisman and throw her arms around his neck. "Ah, Connor, me lad, I knew ye could do it!"

Connor glanced at P.J., who had considerately turned aside to let the siblings celebrate their good fortune. "Aye, but I didn't do it alone, y'know. P.J. helped."

He reached out and drew P.J. to him, gazing down into the eyes of the woman who had saved their lives. Nothing could ever repay that, except, perhaps, devoting his life to her. "I want her to be my wife."

He was rewarded by the shock and joy in P.J.'s face as she registered what he said.

"No!" Stayle exclaimed. "Connor, ye can't! She's a mortal. What about your position?"

"The Fae owe her, Stayle. I owe her, and it's my duty to see the debt's paid. If they can't accept that, then I'm afraid they'll not be having me as their leader anymore."

Stayle shook her head in sorrow. "They'll not countenance their leader having a mortal wife, ye know that. You'll lose your position for certain. What about your dreams, Connor? Your plans for rebuilding the Fae? What about that?"

It was the toughest decision in his life, but he'd made it in an instant, knowing instinctively it was the right thing to do—the only thing to do. "Someone else can do the same, following my plan," he said, knowing it wouldn't work. It was his plan, his vision, his task. No one else could or would follow through on his personal vision.

But that didn't matter now. He'd made his decision and he'd stick to it. Resolutely, he turned away from his sister and looked down into P.J.'s beautiful dark eyes. "'Sure and this isn't blarney, for what I say is true—the luck of the Irish was with me the day that I met you.' P.J., will you marry me?''

P.J. looked back at him, and he knew then he'd always remember her as she was at that moment, staring up at him with hope and love and utter delight.

A flicker of a strange emotion crossed her face, shuttering her gaze. "Oh, Connor, no. I can't."

Connor felt as if he'd been slugged by a troll. "No?"

P.J. glanced at Stayle, who was keeping her mouth shut for a change, letting them work it out. "No," P.J. repeated. "I know how good you are for your people—your first duty is to them. I can't share that with you, and I can't take it away from you."

"But—"

"No, Connor." She pulled away and stared at him dolefully. "Your sister's right. Your people need you, and I'd never forgive myself if I took you away from them. Besides, obligation is no reason to marry." She turned to gather up her things. "I'd better go home."

That stubborn look on her face told him the question was closed—he wasn't going to get anywhere with her now. "All right, P.J., we'll do it your way. But at least give me something to remember you by." He took her into his arms and gave her one last, hard kiss.

Unable to offer her anything else, Connor did the only thing he could. "Goodbye, Petunia Jonquil Sheridan," he whispered, and sent her home with a surge of power.

Behind Connor, Stayle sighed gustily. "Ye did the right thing, Connor."

Connor turned on her. "The right thing! How can you say that?"

" 'Tis best for the Fae, ye know that. And 'tis best for you, as well. She's right, y'know. Obligation is no reason to marry, not if ye don't love her."

"But I do love her!" Connor realized with a blinding flash of insight that it was true. He'd nearly lost P.J. up on that mountain and he didn't ever want to face that again. He loved her, and his life would be lonely and bleak without her. "I do love her," he repeated with more conviction.

Stayle looked skeptical. "Are ye sure about that? She's mortal—not our kind."

"I don't care if she's half elephant! She's good and honest and true—regardless of whether she has magic or no. She's the most important thing in my life, Stayle. I love her, and I'm going to tell her so."

Without his Petunia, life would be flat, boring, desolate—almost as bad as that moment when he'd been sure she was going to die, the gun pressed up against her temple and the shoehorn against her throat.

The shoehorn against her throat? Wait a minute. . . .

Stayle's voice interrupted his musings. "Tell her."

"I'm sorry, what?"

Stayle looked exasperated. "Then go to her now and tell her so."

His incredulity must have showed on his face, for Stayle chuckled and added, "If ye love her, then that's a different story altogether." Her voice softened. "Ye need to follow your heart, Connor me lad."

"But she refused me—you heard her."

"Aye, but only because she thought it was best for you and our people. I'll back ye with the Fae. They'll understand, and if they don't, they'll not be worthy of havin' you as their leader." Stayle placed her hand on his arm. "Go to her, Connor. She loves you, too, y'know—I saw it in her eyes."

He swept her up in a huge bear hug. "Stayle, you're splendid!"

"I know, I know. But let go of me now, ye big oaf, before ye crack me ribs."

He let go of her as requested and she reached up to plant a kiss on his cheek. "Don't mess it up now, hear?"

Connor chuckled. "Nay, this time I won't, but there are two things I need first."

P.J. CLUTCHED THIN AIR as she grasped the space where Connor had been only a moment before. She glanced around in surprise. He'd sent her back to her own bedroom.

P.J. flopped onto her bed and punched the pillow. Damn the man—he hadn't followed the script! He was supposed to plead with her, beg her to be his wife, then assure her he loved her and she wouldn't be ruining the lives of his people.

Oh sure, she'd meant every word when she refused him, but she could have been persuaded.

It was too late now, and she was filled with the numbing realization that he hadn't cared enough to try to change her mind. Instead he'd flicked her home as if she meant absolutely nothing to him.

Bitterly, P.J. remembered Madame Cherelle's prediction. She'd said that at the moment of P.J.'s greatest terror, she had only to make the right decision and she'd have her greatest joy. Well, she'd made the right decision—she'd told Connor her real name. She'd even given him up for the good of his people. So where was the bliss she'd been promised?

"Lass?" came a low voice behind her.

P.J. dashed the tears out of her eyes and turned to stare behind her. "Connor?" Was it really him?

He reached down to pull her up off the bed. "The O'Flahertys don't give up that easily, y'know."

"No?" She hated the quaver in her voice, but she couldn't help it.

"No. I've come to ask you to be my wife—and I won't take no for an answer this time."

Her heart soared. He did care! But she steeled her heart against him—she couldn't let him sacrifice everything he'd worked toward. "You'll have to. You heard what Stayle said. Your people would never forgive you, or me."

"Stayle's changed her mind," Connor said in a soft voice.

"She has?" P.J. said incredulously. "Why?"

"She knows I need you, P.J."

It was P.J.'s turn to inhale sharply. "What do you mean? You have magic . . . you *are* magic. Why would you need me?" Her heart thumped in her rib cage like a wild thing as she waited for his answer.

Connor stroked her cheek and gave her a lazy smile that made her stomach do flip-flops. "I need you to keep my sanity. I need you to laugh with, to love with, to share in good times and bad." He tilted her chin up with his finger. "I need you to have my children. I *need* you to be my wife. Will you marry me?"

"But your people—"

Connor shook his head. "They'll understand, or they'll have to elect another leader. Say yes, P.J."

"But you don't even know my family—"

"I'm sure I'll love them, too. Say yes, P.J."

"But—"

Connor pulled her into his arms and kissed her, silencing her protest. "All that matters is that I love you, lass. Do you love me?"

P.J. nodded dumbly.

Connor grinned in triumph. "Then say yes, P.J."

P.J. glanced around helplessly. *You idiot,* she admonished herself. *This is what you've been waiting for. Say yes, P.J.*

She threw her arms around him. "Yes. Oh, yes!"

Connor whooped and spun her around as if she were a child. He kissed her fiercely, then let go.

"Now there's one more thing I need to know," he said, and pulled Stayle's shoehorn out of his pocket.

Bewildered, P.J. said, "What?"

"Give me your hand, lass."

P.J. did as he asked and watched as he placed the talisman in the palm of her hand. He closed his eyes, murmured a few words in Gaelic, then opened his eyes and grinned.

P.J. stared around herself in wonder. She was surrounded by a field of glittering gold stardust that tinged everything with a hint of magic. She reached out to touch it, but drew back as it faded from view.

She glanced questioningly at Connor and he grinned. " 'Twould seem you've faerie blood in your veins, after all—the aura proves it."

She felt as if she'd been hit by a Mack truck. She was one of the Fae? As Connor stood there grinning, P.J. struggled to take it all in.

"Remember when Neil held the gun to your head and the shoehorn to your throat?"

P.J. shuddered. She preferred not to think about it. "Yes, how could I forget?"

"Well, after you turned me down—" he gave her a mock-disparaging glare "—I remembered you didn't have a rash on your neck from the gold, like you should have."

P.J. nodded slowly, feeling her neck. "That's right. I should have, but I never even noticed."

"Well, that's when I remembered what Madame Cherelle said about your malady."

"What malady?"

"Well, the only one I knew of was your allergy to gold. Something has been niggling at my mind ever since I met you, and I finally remembered what it was—faerie folk who don't believe in magic develop an allergic reaction to their talisman material."

"And when I finally started believing again . . ."

"Then you lost your allergy, I'll be bettin'."

P.J. trembled with excitement. "Do I really have faerie blood?"

Connor reached into his pocket and pulled out a small box. "I made a bet with myself that you did. Here, this is for you."

P.J. opened the box and stared in wonder at the ring nestled there—a gorgeous sparkling square-cut emerald, flanked on either side by the shield of the O'Flaherty clan. She gasped. "It's beautiful."

He took the box gently from her and slipped the ring on the third finger of her left hand. "As are you, lass. 'Tis gold, y'know."

P.J. twisted the ring and admired it. "It's gold," she marveled. "And I don't feel a thing. No insane desire to scratch, no itch, no rash. It's wonderful. How did you know?"

Connor grinned. "I didn't. I only hoped that's what your allergy meant. But it's true, you are one of us."

She was really one of the Fae? Then that meant... she could work magic, too! "What sort of magic do I have, then?"

"The traits are normally hereditary. Let's see." He pressed the shoehorn to her palm again and concentrated as the gold mist coalesced around them once more. "Your father is a leprechaun like me, and your mother is a... pillywiggins."

Suddenly he threw his head back and roared.

"What's so funny?"

He hugged her, continuing to chuckle. "Your mother named you better than she knew. You're half leprechaun, and half flower faerie... Petunia."

She smiled back at him and sighed with happiness when his eyes darkened and he lowered his head, claiming her lips with his.

Her love soared, expanding in ever-widening circles of bliss as the stardust danced around them in a million twinkling points of light, bathing them in the golden glow of their love.

Epilogue

P.J. continued her circuit of the reception hall, her arm tucked securely in her husband's arm. This was her wedding day and she'd never been so happy.

The ceremony, held on the small wooden bridge in Vail where they'd first kissed, had been absolutely beautiful. Wanting to give her the wondrous holiday magic she'd lost many years before, Connor had insisted they marry on Christmas day. The joy of the holiday season and the balmy weather, courtesy of faerie magic, had made it a day to remember.

They'd decided against a formal reception line, preferring to wander about the room and greet their guests individually. Connor linked her fingers with his and eyed the laughing crowd, nodding at one peculiar pairing, whispering, "Who would have thought you'd see those two together?"

Madame Cherelle and Steadman Jarvis stood chatting next to the punch as if they were the best of friends. P.J. chuckled. "I know, and who would have thought Stayle's shoes would have reformed the man so completely? He's become a model citizen and made a mint in the bargain."

Dancers swirled about the room and P.J.'s gaze softened as Patrick Shaughnessy and his wife waltzed by, cheek to cheek, obviously still in love. "I hope we'll be like them in twenty years."

Connor squeezed her hand. "We will be, lass, we will be. And speaking of odd pairings, here's another one for you."

Stayle and Amaranth strolled up, arm in arm, chattering away as if they were the best of friends. They were, too, now that Stayle was teaching Amaranth magic.

P.J. just shook her head. Ever since her family had learned they were faerie, they'd realized what they'd been searching for all their lives and had entered wholeheartedly into the life of the Fae, including magic lessons. Her father had proven an apt pupil and was even now showing the Magnificent Ambrose a trick or two on the other side of the room. P.J. took after her father and was fast perfecting her own glamarye to help in her investigative reporting.

Her mother, living up to her pillywiggins name, had discovered a bent for growing flowers magically and had delighted in showing off her new powers by providing a profusion of fresh blooms for the wedding.

Amaranth had shown a remarkable aptitude for growing things, as well. But, not to anyone's surprise, she preferred to concentrate on fruit. She'd contributed her skills to the wedding, too, and exotic fresh fruit interspersed with ordinary apples and oranges lay piled in enormous pyramids around the room.

P.J. and Connor turned to greet their sisters, and Stayle smiled at them. " 'Tis a lovely weddin', P.J., and you're a lovely bride."

P.J. smiled back at her, liking her new sister-in-law now that she'd regained her talisman. "Thank you, and thank you also for my wonderful shoes." P.J. lifted her long white dress and held out her foot, gazing in appreciation once more at the beautiful, elegant shoes Stayle had designed for her.

Stayle had outdone herself this time. Made of a supple white leather that never seemed to scratch or mar, the pumps had a tiny print that consisted of the initials of her name intertwined with Connor's. Three dainty straps arched diagonally across her instep to meet high on the low-cut toe, providing tantalizing glimpses of the skin beneath. The heel cup flowed into the shoe in an elegant undulating line that made her look soft and feminine, yet competent and sure of herself. And as a crowning touch, the straps were anchored in place by a single delicate diamond-studded heart.

The shoes gave the overall impression of a sensible, classy career woman who had a touch of whimsy and love, if you only looked close enough. Charmed anew, P.J. said, "Is this really how you see me?"

"Nay, 'tis how you are," Stayle said, then hugged her.

P.J. smiled. "Thank you. I feel very lucky to have a pair of Stayle O'Flaherty shoes." She glanced around. "And it appears most of the people here feel the same—there are very few without them."

"Aye, due primarily to that wonderful article ye wrote about me store. I've had more business than I know what to do with. Thank you again, and the best of luck to ye.''

Stayle stepped back and let Amaranth come forward. Tears filled P.J.'s eyes as her sister gave her a fierce hug and whispered, "You'll be happy, I know you will.''

These past couple of months, P.J. had come to know her sister better than she ever had before. Strangely, learning she had magic of her own had brought Amaranth down from the clouds, and they found they had a lot more in common than they'd thought. That was another blessing she had to thank Connor for.

P.J. glanced up at her husband and returned his smile. "I know we will, too.''

Amaranth looked up at Connor. "There's just one thing that puzzles me.''

"What's that?" Connor asked.

She nodded toward the dance floor, where Melissa and Neil danced past Bernard and the Irish innkeeper. "Of all people, why'd you pick Neil Chalmers as your best man?''

Connor chuckled deep in his throat. "Well, he did bring us together, after all.''

Amaranth just shook her head in bewilderment and walked away. The dance ended, and Jarvis claimed Melissa for the next dance. Now minus a dancing partner, Neil strode over to shake Connor's hand. "Man, I can't thank you enough.''

"It was nothing.''

"No," Neil insisted. "It wasn't. If it weren't for those boggarts you sent after me, I'd probably still be stuck in my own private hell.''

Curious to hear the whole story, P.J. asked, "What do you mean?"

Neil lowered his voice. "Well, after Connor magicked me away to that jail cell, he could have done anything he liked with me. Instead, he chose to cure me, and am I glad he did! After a few nasty moments, the boggarts realized the kleptomania was a recent thing—a spell—so they called Connor."

"A spell?" P.J. echoed.

"Aye," Connor said. "It seems Neil here angered the elves when he wrote his screenplay depicting them as nasty, cold creatures, so they laid this spell on him to discredit him."

"So how did you cure him?"

"Well, I sent Stayle to him, to give him a pair of shoes, though he didn't much care for the idea at first."

Neil turned red. "You got that right. I didn't know what she was going to do and her magic terrified me. I was kicking and screaming so hard, she had to call some trolls to sit on me. I felt pretty silly when all she did was force some shoes on my feet."

P.J. chuckled. "Well, I'm glad that everything came out all right in the end."

Neil nodded vehemently. "I'll say it did. They cured me. And, say, I'm sorry about treating you the way I did. I—I wasn't myself. Can you forgive me?"

She smiled. "Yes, of course. You were under the influence of the elves' spell—you didn't have any choice."

Neil nodded in relief. "Yes, and now Connor's convinced some of them to advise me on the film, to make sure I've got it right. It's gonna be great. Make sure you see it."

They promised to do so, and Neil said his goodbyes and left.

P.J. glanced around the room. "Connor, our guests are having a wonderful time and they don't really need us. Do you think we could slip away and...start our honeymoon a little early?" She couldn't wait to have him all to herself in that little Irish valley he'd purchased for their people.

"Aye, lass, but first there's someone else who wants to talk to us." He nodded at Madame Cherelle, who was slowly making her way to their side.

"Bonjour," Madame Cherelle said. "I can see you are leaving so I won't keep you long. I just wanted to give you your wedding gift, *ma petite.*"

"That's not necessary—" P.J. began.

"Ah, but it is," Madame said. "Please, hold out your hand."

Remembering the last time Madame had read her future, P.J. was a little reluctant, but Connor encouraged her with a wink and a nod.

With a sigh, P.J. gave Madame her hand and Madame placed her amethyst talisman against it, closing her eyes as she concentrated on seeing P.J.'s future.

After a few minutes Madame's lips curved in a smile and she dropped P.J.'s hand.

"What did you see?" P.J. asked.

"Congratulations. You and your new husband will be very happy. Within the year, Connor will get his wish for new additions to the Fae."

Joy welled up within P.J. "You mean...we're going to have a baby?" she asked in awe.

Madame Cherelle shook her head. "No, *ma petite.* Not *a* baby. Three of them. You're going to have triplets!"

BRIDE'S BAY RESORT

UNLOCK THE DOOR TO GREAT ROMANCE
AT BRIDE'S BAY RESORT

Join Harlequin's new across-the-lines series, set
in an exclusive hotel on an island off the coast of
South Carolina.

Seven of your favorite authors will bring you exciting stories
about fascinating heroes and heroines discovering love at
Bride's Bay Resort.

Look for these fabulous stories coming to a store near you
beginning in January 1996.

Harlequin American Romance #613 in January
Matchmaking Baby by Cathy Gillen Thacker

Harlequin Presents #1794 in February
Indiscretions by Robyn Donald

Harlequin Intrigue #362 in March
Love and Lies by Dawn Stewardson

Harlequin Romance #3404 in April
Make Believe Engagement by Day Leclaire

Harlequin Temptation #588 in May
Stranger in the Night by Roseanne Williams

Harlequin Superromance #695 in June
Married to a Stranger by Connie Bennett

Harlequin Historicals #324 in July
Dulcie's Gift by Ruth Langan

Visit Bride's Bay Resort each month wherever
Harlequin books are sold.

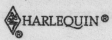

HARLEQUIN ®

BBAYG

IT'S A BABY BOOM!

NEW ARRIVALS

We're expecting—again! Join us for the New Arrivals promotion, in which special American Romance authors invite you to read about equally special heroines—all of whom are on a nine-month adventure! We expect each mom-to-be will find the man of her dreams—and a daddy in the bargain!

Watch for the newest arrival. Due date: next month...

#617 THE BOUNTY HUNTER'S BABY
by Jule McBride
February 1996

NA-4

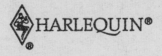

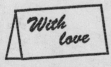

This February, watch how
three tough guys handle the

Baby
BEAT

Lieutenant Jake Cameron, Detective Cole Bennett and
Agent Seth Norris fight crime and put their lives on the
line every day. Now they're changing diapers, talking
baby talk and wheeling strollers.

Nobody told them there'd be days like this....

Three complete novels by some of your favorite
authors—in one special collection!

TIGERS BY NIGHT by Sandra Canfield
SOMEONE'S BABY by Sandra Kitt
COME HOME TO ME by Marisa Carroll

Available wherever Harlequin and Silhouette books are sold.

HARLEQUIN ® *Silhouette*®

HRE0296

When desires run wild,

can be deadly

JoAnn Ross

The shocking murder of a senator's beautiful wife
has shaken the town of Whiskey River. Town sheriff
Trace Callihan gets more than he bargained for when the
victim's estranged sister, Mariah Swann, insists on being
involved with the investigation.

As the black sheep of the family returning from Hollywood,
Mariah has her heart set on more than just solving her
sister's death, and Trace, a former big-city cop, has more
on his mind than law and order.

What will transpire when dark secrets and suppressed
desires are unearthed by this unlikely pair? Because nothing
is as it seems in Whiskey River—and everyone is a suspect.

Look for *Confessions* at your favorite retail outlet this January.

MJRC

<u>MIRA</u> The brightest star in women's fiction